HARLEQUIN®
Presents

What do you love most about reading Harlequin Presents books? From what you tell us, it's our sexy foreign heroes, exciting and emotionally intense relationships, generous helpings of pure passion and glamorous international settings that bring you pleasure!

Welcome to February 2007's stunning selection of eight novels that bring you emotion, passion and excitement galore, as you are whisked around the world to meet men who make love in many languages. And you'll also find your favorite authors: Penny Jordan, Lucy Monroe, Kate Walker, Susan Stephens, Sandra Field, Carole Mortimer, Elizabeth Power and Anne McAllister.

Sit back and let us entertain you....

Susan Stephens

THE GREEK'S
BRIDAL PURCHASE

HARLEQUIN®

TORONTO • NEW YORK • LONDON
AMSTERDAM • PARIS • SYDNEY • HAMBURG
STOCKHOLM • ATHENS • TOKYO • MILAN • MADRID
PRAGUE • WARSAW • BUDAPEST • AUCKLAND

ISBN-13: 978-0-373-12606-4
ISBN-10:   0-373-12606-9

THE GREEK'S BRIDAL PURCHASE

First North American Publication 2007.

Copyright © 2006 by Susan Stephens.

This edition published by arrangement with Harlequin Books S.A.

® and TM are trademarks of the publisher. Trademarks indicated with ® are registered in the United States Patent and Trademark Office, the Canadian Trade Marks Office and in other countries.

www.eHarlequin.com

Printed in U.S.A.

All about the author…
Susan Stephens

SUSAN STEPHENS was a professional
singer before meeting her husband on the tiny
Mediterranean island of Malta. In true Harlequin
Presents style they met on Monday, became
engaged on Friday and were married three
months later. Almost thirty years and three
children later they are still in love. (Susan does
not advise her children to return home one day
with a similar story as she may not take the news
with the same fortitude as her own mother!)

Susan had written several nonfiction books when
fate took a hand. At a charity costume ball there
was an after-dinner auction. One of the lots,
"Spend a Day with an Author," had been donated
by Harlequin Presents author Penny Jordan.
Susan's husband bought this lot and Penny was to
become not just a great friend, but a wonderful
mentor who encouraged Susan to write romance.

Susan loves her family, her pets, her friends and
her writing. She enjoys entertaining, travel and
going to the theater. She reads, cooks and plays
the piano to relax, and can occasionally be found
throwing herself off mountains on a pair of skis
or galloping through the countryside.

Visit Susan's website at www.susanstephens.net.
She loves to hear from her readers all around the
world!

PROLOGUE

'It's time you found a wife, Theo. You have responsibilities. If you agree, I will transfer my controlling interest of the Savakis shipping line to you upon my death. If you refuse, I sign this.'

'This' was a document that would consign the company to the greed of the old man's remaining cronies on the board, Theo Savakis realised, holding the stare of his grandfather, Dimitri.

Dimitri had been a chairman in the old style, squandering his wealth and caring little for the welfare of his people. Was Theo to lose everything he had built up during his tenure as acting chairman at the whim of such a man? Should he stand back and see the company slump back into ruin, the people he cared about thrown out of work? Or should he do as Dimitri wanted: marry a virgin and breed from her?

'You leave me no choice.'

'Don't sound so bitter, Theo. What am I asking of you— that you should go find a young girl? Is that so much?'

His grandfather's gesture made Theo's stomach clench with disgust. The wheedling he was accustomed to, but the cynical use of women as breeding stock, the dynastic marriages that so often failed between prominent Greek families?

Those he would never embrace. '*Theos*, Dimitri! This is the twenty-first century—'

'Exactly.' The old schemer cut across him. 'Where would you get such a bargain today? All I'm asking for is your signature, Theo. And for that you get your own shipping line, with a woman thrown in.'

His grandfather's domineering personality had broken his father's spirit, driving Acteon Savakis into a life of self-indulgence. That would never happen to him, Theo had vowed silently. After his parents had been killed in a tragic accident he had seized the helm of the Savakis shipping line and devoted his working life to rebuilding the company into a world-class business. His grandfather had retained a controlling interest, and if Theo was to realise his vision for the future he had to inherit those golden shares. To achieve this it appeared he must commit to a marriage before he had even identified a bride.

'I want my name to live on, Theo,' Dimitri wheedled. 'Is that so hard for you to understand?'

Hard to understand? No. Dimitri's life had been entirely self-focused. But it was Theo's family name too, and he was damned if he would allow the Savakis shipping line to fall into the hands of his grandfather's sycophants. 'I will sign,' he agreed. 'On one condition. *I* choose the mother of my child, Dimitri. *I* choose my bride.'

'No.' The old man shook his head. 'I have already found you a woman.'

'A virgin?'

'Cut the cynicism, Theo. Lexis Chandris is the daughter of my closest friend.'

As good a reason as any to refuse, Theo mused as his grandfather opened his arms wide.

'At least give her a trial…'

'A trial?'

'Don't play the innocent with me, Theo. Take her to bed, and—'

'Yes—thank you.' He silenced Dimitri with a glance.

'Her father has already sent her to Kalmos—'

'He's *what*?'

'I told him you were intending to take the yacht there, and that it would be a good opportunity for you to take another look at her. Surely you can see the advantage of making such a marriage? I'm talking about the daughter of another shipping family. Together the two companies will form an impregnable empire. You can't avoid your fate, Theo. This is your destiny!'

'No, Dimitri. I make my own path through life.'

Theo held his grandfather's stare until it faltered, and Dimitri shrugged. 'Well… But if you want me to sign over my shares you must settle on a woman before I die.'

'That may not be possible.'

'Not good enough, Theo.'

The fate of the Savakis shipping line was hanging in the balance. 'Very well. I give you my word.'

'Excellent. Lexis won't be wasted. I hear she's beautiful, but if she's not to your taste just use her and send her back.'

Theo stared at his grandfather in disbelief. Each time he thought Dimitri had plumbed the depths, he managed to surprise him. 'Is this how you treat the children of your friends?'

'You're too soft, Theo.'

'Really?' Theo wondered how well Dimitri knew him. He might have been brought up beneath his grandfather's roof after the death of his parents, but they were still strangers to each other.

'Remember,' Dimitri cautioned, 'if you shun this girl you must find another before I die. But stay away from trouble.

No artistic types, no Cinderellas, and no worthy causes. I see you looking at me with distaste, Theo, but you and I are from the same mould—destined for greater things than hearth and home. Some women understand that—my friend's daughter would understand that. Other women look for something more, something we can never give them.'

'And what's that?'

'Love, Theo. Now, will you sign?' Dimitri Savakis pushed the relevant document across the desk.

Uncapping his fountain pen, Theo signed below his grandfather's signature, adding the date, and then, for the last time, he shook Dimitri's hand.

CHAPTER ONE

KALMOS. A tiny island, set like a gem in the Aegean. Perfect.

Miranda leaned over the rail as the ferry reversed its engines and drifted slowly into port. It had taken an age, but, however slow and primitive the inter-island ferry might be, it was better than trusting her life to the small turbo-prop aircraft that made the same journey. Her knees were still knocking after the flight to Athens.

She was in a crowd of maybe twenty people waiting to disembark, the only pale and silent stranger in a cheery mob of smiling faces. The sun gave you licence to raise your voice, to laugh out loud, to catch someone's eye and greet them like a friend...

'Oh, no, thank you, I can manage!' She dragged her roll-along suitcase a little closer as an elderly man tried to help her with it. He took it anyway.

She waited for the familiar anger to surge up inside her, and then realised she wasn't angry. Well, that was a start. Anger was such a destructive emotion. If she couldn't lose the anger she would never heal inside, and those wounds were far more serious than the damage to her arm.

Thinking she was behind him, the man had already lifted her bag and walked away. She caught up with him onshore.

'*Efharisto*. Thank you.' She smiled, practising one of the essentials she had picked up in her phrasebook.

'*Parakolo*.'

Still beaming, he turned back to his group after returning her courtesy.

He was intent on his family, she noticed, and suffused with the type of joy that made her feel wistful. She had cut herself off from her own family. She had lied to them. She had said she would teach for a short while—just until she regained full use of her arm.

'*Adio*,' he called, waving as she walked away.

'*Adio*,' Miranda called back. It was such a thrill not to be stared at, or to be treated any differently.

Miranda Weston, world-class violinist. She had led a charmed life up to the accident. Afterwards she had become an embarrassment, usually discussed in the third person, as if her hearing had gone along with her ability to make music.

She had never been weak; she couldn't afford to be. You couldn't show a tender underbelly in the world of classical musicians—not unless you wanted it ripped out. But the accident had stripped all her confidence away. She'd lost so much. She had been faced with two options: to stay in London, where everyone knew her, or to leave the country and start again, one building block at a time.

The irony was that what had allowed her to make this trip were the royalties for her one and only CD, which had landed on the doormat at just the right moment. She had been hugging herself in a huddle of misery at her apartment, curtains still drawn against another unwelcome day. But when she'd read the cheque she had been forced to count the noughts three times. *How* many copies had she sold?

That had been the turning point, when she had decided to get away—partly to avoid telling a family that had sacrificed so much for her about the latest prognosis on her ruined arm, but more in an attempt to redefine herself and find new purpose and direction for her life. Perhaps she couldn't be an international violinist, but she had to be *someone*. She couldn't just step off the bandwagon altogether.

The tiny Greek island of Kalmos was far enough away for people not to know who she was or who she had been. And she was attracted to the sunshine, the sea and the swimming— something she could still do, and *had* to do if she wanted to improve the movement in her arm.

As people started to drift away from the quay Miranda gave a happy sigh and turned her face up to the sun, revelling in the knowledge that at last she was free. Free from the past and free from those who wanted to manipulate her. She was still stinging from memories of her own Svengali figure, the manager who had directed her career only to try and turn her into a sob-story for the tabloids when she was no longer any use to him. And she was still suffering from nightmares after the accident that had destroyed a lot more than a career.

But she would not sit back and let others cast her in the role of victim. She would rebuild her life, but on her own terms. And one very good way to make a start was to locate her apartment, unpack, and find a job. That was her target for today.

Tomorrow, the world…

This was as close to perfect as it got. She had a sea-front balcony, and the sea was an improbable shade of blue. The sky was even bluer, if that was possible; in fact all the colours seemed a little brighter here on the island.

She had chosen Kalmos because the girl at the travel agent had said it was the most picturesque and least commercialised of all the Greek islands. Well, it was certainly beautiful, and her simple apartment was in a prime location. Set in a small block, it was in the centre of a long sugar-sand beach. And, just as she'd hoped, there was a taverna within walking distance.

She'd travelled light, knowing she wouldn't need much in a hot climate, but she had brought a couple of special outfits just in case she found some singing work. When she had been a student at the music *conservatoire* she had brought in extra money by singing with a band. It hadn't paid too well, but she'd usually got a free meal as part of the deal.

And if she couldn't get work as a singer she would take any job. She felt sure that whatever happened would give her a whole new view on life. It wasn't everyone who got the chance to start over with a clean sheet.

Miranda's optimism took flight. Her twin, Emily, had met her prince the night a dose of flu had kept Miranda in bed, putting Emily on stage in her place. One night was all it took…

Yes, but get real, Miranda, she told herself. *Lightning never strikes twice in the same place. And even if it does, it's life, and it's up to me to sort it out.* Even Prince Charming waiting in the wings couldn't change her mind about that.

Quickly twisting her long black hair into a respectable coil, she pulled on a jade green T-shirt the same colour as her eyes. Satisfied that she was ready for her first job interview, she added a slick of lipgloss and grabbed her bag.

The golden sunlight embraced her the moment she stepped outside. Miranda could feel all her tension easing away as she slipped sunglasses onto her nose and shifted the strap of her bag containing music and all the other paraphernalia associated with auditions. She had no idea what to expect, and it wasn't easy to strike a balance between, *Yes, I would love to sing for you*, and, *Yes, washing up sounds perfect*, when it came to achieving the right look.

She had gone for understated, wearing what she imagined

would become her daytime uniform: plain top, cropped pants and flip-flops. Flip-flops because she had to walk across the sand to her first job interview. Who wouldn't be smiling?

It didn't take Miranda long to discover that a nut-brown friendly individual named Spiros owned the taverna.

'And this is my wife, Agalia.'

'Miranda.' Miranda smiled back at Agalia, who was just as round and sunny as her husband. She had a feeling everything was going to be all right. The couple's welcome was so warm, and it wasn't long before Spiros was offering her a job. Waiting on tables, singing, working behind the bar—anything, as and when required, he said.

Concerned about letting him down, Miranda quickly explained that she might not be quite as dextrous as the rest of his staff and might be better off in the kitchen. Spiros only made a dismissive gesture, barely glancing at her hand. The pay was minimal, but the clientele was rarely demanding, he reassured her, and, above all, she was their friend and a welcome guest to the island.

She needed this like oxygen, Miranda realised. Real people—people without an agenda, people who didn't know the celebrity she had briefly been. Out here on Kalmos she was just someone else on the brink of life, testing what the world had to offer before the weight of responsibility tied her down. It was all the therapy she needed. She could feel the tension easing from her shoulders, and smiled happily when Spiros and Agalia suggested she should join them for lunch.

'I can't think of anything I'd like more,' she said eagerly.

'You must be tired after your journey?' Agalia suggested, passing a dish of plump green olives and a basket of freshly baked bread.

'No, not at all.' It was true, Miranda discovered. She was infused with life already, as if friendship and sunshine had washed warmth through her veins. 'I haven't felt so good for such a long time.' She blushed, noticing her blunt admission had cast a shadow over the faces of her hosts. 'To Kalmos,' she added brightly, determined to restore the mood again as she raised her glass in a toast.

'To you, Miranda,' Spiros and Agalia chorused warmly, exchanging the briefest of glances before chinking glasses with her.

The moment she woke the next morning Miranda was overwhelmed by disappointment and frustration. The nightmare had come back. She had hoped the change of scene would help, but here she was, tense and trembling, because of the deep-laid guilt that was her constant shadow. Maybe she would never escape…

But if that were the case she had to learn to live with it and get on with her life, or the guilt would destroy her.

Swimming. Yawning, she stretched. That was what she would do. She would fight the mental demons with exercise. She loved swimming, she was good at it, and it was essential if her arm was to improve at all.

She had been swimming every day back home, to try and strengthen it, and here she had the chance to ease the tight muscles of her hand in the healing waters of the sea. The ugly red scars had faded a little since the accident, but her fingers were still awkwardly bent, and her arm hadn't straightened properly either. It was always a little stiff to start with, but if she had to undergo physiotherapy anywhere, Kalmos was the place.

Heading for the water, Miranda tested the temperature with her toes and found it warm. She had always been a good swimmer, confident too, and this was one thing she had really been looking forward to.

She hit the current when she was about a hundred yards

out from the shore. There was no tell-tale sign, no gradual tug on her legs—nothing to alert her at all. It came fast, like so many watery hands, pulling her out to sea. For a few seconds she panicked, and started flailing around, but then she relaxed into the drag, keeping her head above water to try and work out how to steer herself to safety, or find something to grab on to—a rock, an anchor chain, anything…

Then, just as suddenly, the current spewed her out into calmer waters. She picked a course back with greater care, taking a route that would take her closer to the moored boats. She had learned a valuable lesson, and would show the unpredictable current more respect in future.

When she first heard the whine of a high-powered engine she had no idea that the speedboat was heading straight for her. The moment she realised, she shot up an arm to warn of her presence in the water. She caught a glimpse of a man standing up in the bow, and then he slewed the boat around, swamping her in the wash. The next thing she knew he was dragging her on board, and she was coughing up seawater on his deck.

'There are dangerous currents between these two islands. What did you think you were you doing?'

The deep and very masculine voice was like a rasp on metal, and about as welcome as a curse. She couldn't talk and choke at the same time, which held her back from stating the obvious. She put out her good hand to shut him up.

'*Vlakas*!'

'I beg your pardon?' She hadn't a clue what he had said, but knew it wasn't nice. Rather than showing remorse after swearing at her, the man gave another, equally scathing sound of contempt as he tossed a heavy towel across her shoulders.

Miranda dragged it around her shoulders, taking a moment to recover from the shock. Then, shading her eyes, she gazed up. The man drew himself a little taller.

'You people stop at nothing, do you?'

He sounded so hostile. 'Do we know each other?' she enquired coldly.

'I expect you know me from a newscast, or from some journal.'

'Oh, really?' She pressed her lips together, trying not to smile. The situation was suddenly very funny. The man must be someone famous—but who was he? She didn't have a clue. It appeared they both feared the consequences of fame, and were both mistaken in imagining their celebrity had found a worldwide audience. It made her feel better. In fact, it made her feel great.

'So what is this?' He glanced around suspiciously. 'A set-up?'

'A set-up?' She struggled into a sitting position. 'What are you talking about?'

'The rescue…was it a device to get a good photograph?' He scanned the shore. 'Where's your cameraman?'

'Are you insane?' She choked back a laugh.

'So this is just a coincidence?' he asked sarcastically.

He was really quite stunning, she saw now, but that was no excuse for his behaviour. 'A coincidence?' she repeated. 'What do you mean?'

'*Vlakas!*' he muttered again, apparently on the edge of fury.

She cooled rapidly at his tone. 'Right. First of all, I didn't need rescuing. And secondly—'

'What?'

'Secondly, don't bark at me!' That wasn't what she had intended to say, but she didn't like his tone of voice; she didn't like the arrogant way his feet were planted on the deck; she didn't like the way he was towering over her.

'You're lucky I was around to bark at you. I might have been dragging your lifeless body off my anchor chain instead.'

And then, before she could answer him, he added, 'How long have you been watching me?'

'Watching you? I had no idea you were so fascinating.'

'Oh, so you didn't notice my yacht?' His turn for sarcasm.

Following the pointing finger, Miranda blenched. There it was, a huge white monstrosity, sleekly sensational and totally unmissable, though from her apartment she might not have seen it. 'I didn't see it—and anyway, how would I have known it was yours?'

'The same way you recognised me, I imagine…from some tawdry magazine.'

Anger shot her to her knees, then to her feet, and at the sudden movement the small craft rocked perilously beneath her, throwing her against him, flesh on flesh, brief, warm, frightening. She pulled away fast.

'You'll have us both in the sea!' He roared the words, planting his legs apart like some rampaging pirate, straddling the deck to steady the boat with sheer brute strength.

'You're yelling at me? When you almost drowned me?' She planted her hands on her hips. 'What the hell did you think you were doing, turning your boat around in the water so quickly like that?'

'Trying to save you! You nearly drowned through your own stupidity. I had to act quickly before you were dragged under again. Didn't you think to ask about the currents before you went into the sea?'

'*Excuse* me?' She was ready for battle, but it wasn't easy doing battle with a bronzed opponent wearing nothing but clingy black swimming shorts and a diver's watch.

'Idiot!' He glared down at her.

The distraction wore off fast. She suspected he was translating, in case she hadn't got the message that he'd been insulting her before. 'So, who the hell are you?'

'Theo Savakis,' he said, with a gust of disdain. 'As if you didn't know.'

'Well, I didn't know. But now that I do—is *idiot* your favourite word, Mr Savakis? Or is it just that your vocabulary's rather limited?'

That stalled him.

'And now, if you've quite finished, I'd like you to take me back,' she added, gesturing towards the shore.

To her surprise, his lips quirked at one corner—as if he wanted to laugh, as if it was the first time anyone had ever spoken to him that way. But he quickly got over it and hardened his expression.

'Now would be good.' She drummed her fingers on the side.

'Before we do that you might want to...' He dipped his head rather than elaborating, and then she discovered that one of her breasts had parted company with the top half of her bikini. Tilting her chin a little higher, to stare him in the eyes, she made the necessary adjustment. But holding his gaze was a mistake. She hadn't expected such humour. And he did have very beautiful eyes: grey, with extremely white whites, and the pewter-grey iris was rimmed in pitch-black, like his hair...

'The shore?' she reminded him, but unfortunately her voice came out as more of a squeak than at the volume she had intended.

'When I'm ready...'

A flutter of alarm spread outwards from Miranda's heart as Theo Savakis continued to stare at her. Firm mouth, uncompromising bearing, and showing not the slightest intention of allowing her to stare him down. He didn't have a melting point anywhere. And, in spite of not liking him, she liked that.

'That arm looks sore. Have you seen a doctor?'

Now she was completely thrown. No one talked about her injury. Most people turned away, too embarrassed even to admit its existence.

'Several. Can we go now?' Instinctively she moved her shoulder back, hiding the worst of the damaged area by angling her body—something she'd become rather good at.

He seemed lost in thought as he narrowed his eyes. 'Like I said, when I'm ready.'

Was he trying to place her? Not a chance, Miranda realised thankfully. No one knew her here in Kalmos. The chance of this brute remembering her fleeting appearance on the world stage was as unlikely as slicing a loaf of bread with a banana. As far as he was concerned she was just one more tourist, lowering the tone of his precious island. He would soon forget this incident, and file her away with the rest of the trash.

'I know you…'

Her look of blank disbelief was greeted by an infuriatingly confident smile. And as colour raged into her cheeks he rasped a thumb across some early-morning stubble.

'All right, I forgive you. I guess you weren't looking for a scoop. But I must admit I'm a little confused as to what you're doing here on Kalmos.'

'Only a little?' Miranda drew herself up. He was mistaken. He couldn't possibly know who she was.

'Aren't you the violinist Miranda Weston?'

CHAPTER TWO

'I *WAS* the violinist Miranda Weston.'

'Of course. Your arm...'

And then he didn't just glance at it and look away. He gave it a good long stare, as if assessing the level of damage. 'I seem to remember reading something. It must have been a serious accident?'

His words echoed through her, bringing all the horrors of the nightmare back. His blatant disregard for convention was hard to believe. No one discussed a serious injury with a stranger. Theo Savakis should have known that. He had no right to be so blunt. He should have shown more control, more consideration for her feelings, more sensitivity—

'What are you doing here in Kalmos, Miranda? Recuperating?'

She made a noncommittal sound. She wanted to be out of the spotlight. She didn't want to answer his questions. She didn't want to be drawn into conversation by someone whose very wholeness and vigour was like a distorting mirror at a fairground, that reflected her disfigurement and made it seem more pronounced.

'You couldn't have chosen anywhere better to recuperate than Kalmos—'

'I'm getting cold.' She spoke churlishly, not caring what he thought of her manner.

Turning away to the controls, he put his hand on a lever and moved it out of neutral. He opened up the throttle, and pointed the slim fast craft towards the shore.

She didn't speak on the ride back. It would have been impossible anyway against the noise of the engine. She waded in the last few yards to shore, after he'd helped her over the side of the boat, feeling horribly exposed in her skimpy bikini, and almost brandishing her injuries under his nose like a warning to leave her alone. She didn't think she had much to worry about, though. His type avoided imperfections as though they were catching.

But on the walk back to her apartment Miranda felt an ache growing inside her. Theo Savakis hadn't looked at her in the way a man looked at a woman when he wanted her in his bed. But why would he want her, when she was angry and touchy—damaged inside as well as out?

And now she was feeling sorry for herself again, which was everything she had vowed to leave behind.

It was absurd to feel like that! Theo Savakis was possibly the most obnoxious individual on the planet. And yet, in spite of that, she did feel something for him…a tingle? More like a full-throated roar! Under the circumstances, that was nothing short of amazing—because she hated sex. She'd only tried it once, and that had been a disaster. It had hurt, and had made her feel like an object. She had stared at the wall until it was over. She could still remember the peeling paint in the student bedsit…

Theo's touch had been firm and warm. Safe? She couldn't say, but at least it had been completely impersonal.

When Miranda closed the door of the apartment behind her she sighed with relief. So much had happened, and it was good to be alone. She had thought her time on Kalmos would allow for a slow healing process, conducted to the sound of seagulls and lapping waves. She had not expected to be thrown into a full-scale drama with a man like Theo Savakis.

But at least the incident had proved one thing. She was daring to tap into emotion again.

Miranda threw all her energies into preparing for her first day's work at the taverna. She showered and dressed quickly, tying back her hair and not bothering with make-up, telling herself she was going to forget Theo Savakis. She was going to love working at the taverna. She could feel it in her bones. And no one was going to spoil it for her.

'*Oy!* Miranda! It's great to see you!'

Spiros looked up as she approached the wooden jetty where he was washing down tables.

'Would you like me to do that for you?' she said, running up the steps.

'You can help me if you like.' Dipping into his bucket, he squeezed out a second cloth and handed it to her. They started working companionably in the same easy rhythm.

'We're having a party tonight,' Spiros told her when they had finished. 'I know it's short notice, but would you sing for us, Miranda?'

She had offered to sing, she had even come to Kalmos hoping to sing, but all Miranda could think now was that she hadn't been in the spotlight since the accident. She hadn't sung in public since her student days, which in fairness weren't so very far behind her—eighteen months, two years, perhaps. Her professional career had been so short...

'If you'd rather not, I understand. We have a *bouzouki* band, so there will be music during the evening. It's up to you, Miranda.' Cocking his head to one side, Spiros waited for her answer.

'Of course I'll sing for you.' How could she possibly let him down? And she had no intention of hiding away for the rest of her life either. 'I brought some backing tapes with me, and a dress. I'd love to sing for you, Spiros.'

'That's settled, then.'

'And I'll come over early tonight, so that I can help you in the kitchen, too.'

'You're like a member of my family already,' Spiros declared happily. 'And tonight you'll meet some more of my relatives. It will be like one big, happy family.' He beamed at her. 'Why don't we go and see what Agalia has prepared for our breakfast?'

She dressed simply that evening, in clean Capri pants with a loose white shirt over the top. She wanted to be comfortable, and Spiros had told her that none of the staff at the taverna wore a uniform. Most of them were relatives, she understood, marvelling at the size of Spiros's family. She packed a dress as well, something she could wear for singing, as well as some decent shoes, and put everything, including her backing tapes, into a large soft bag.

Standing on the balcony before she left, she felt a rush of excitement. She could hear the taverna springing to life; she could hear rolling waves mingling with the conversation. Gathering her long hair into a loose ponytail at the nape of her neck, she smiled with anticipation.

Once she was outside, she slipped off her sandals and picked her way across the cool, damp sand. It was a romantic way to go to work, and there was even a full moon, Miranda noticed, gazing skywards. Anyone on earth would have envied her at that moment. And she was lucky. People got killed in car accidents like the one she'd had, but she had been given a second chance—and she wasn't going to waste it.

But when she drew closer Miranda's mouth dried as she saw how many people were piling into the taverna. Was this Spiros's idea of a family reunion? But then he *did* have a rather large family, she remembered wryly. Even so, she had been expecting a party, not a stadium event! She had envisaged a low-key gathering, which would have given her the opportunity, after so long an absence, to mount the stage and sing a few songs without any pressure.

How wrong could you be? There were dozens of cars in the car park, and headlights were still streaming in procession down the hill!

Keeping to the shadows beneath the jetty, she took her time brushing sand off her feet. Anything to put off the moment when she had to walk into the light and be noticed...

'Miranda—there you are! Come and join us!'

As Spiros hurried down the steps to greet her Miranda came out of the shadows, feeling ashamed that she had been hiding.

Spiros kissed her continental fashion, on both cheeks, and then put his arm around her shoulders, reaching for her heavy bag at the same time. 'You don't know how much we appreciate this, Miranda.' Drawing her with him, he steered her through the crowds already massing in the main body of the taverna. 'Isn't this wonderful!'

As Spiros turned to her, Miranda's tension relaxed into a laugh. If chaos was wonderful, then this was superb!

'How could you fail to feel on top of the world with people like these around you?' Spiros demanded, enthusiastically shouldering open the door into the kitchen. 'This is a very special night for us, Miranda.'

As people glanced up from their tasks to smile, Miranda knew Spiros was right. This wasn't a big city, and she wasn't about to face some critical gathering of classical groupies; this was Kalmos, where life was simple and good.

And yet she was still feeling apprehensive. Which was ridiculous, she told herself firmly. What on earth did she have to be apprehensive about?

It was hot working behind the scenes at the taverna; hot, but good-humoured, and ear-shatteringly noisy. Each time the swing door flipped open for a moment Miranda saw that every age group was represented outside, from the oldest folk in the village to babes in arms. Children were allowed to run free, dodging under the tables and weaving in and out of tightly packed groups, causing even more disruption. But no one seemed to mind, and no one called out rudely to any of the waiting staff. In fact people were just as likely to follow them into the kitchen, choose something to eat, and then help the waiters carry the plates of food back to their table.

'Come and meet my family,' Spiros insisted, shepherding her outside during a brief lull in the proceedings. Resplendent in a crisp white shirt and a bright red waistcoat, heavily embroidered with gold, he looked every bit the proud and successful restaurateur. Agalia, Miranda had learned, preferred her position as kitchen general. Nothing went through the doors without her say-so.

'*Ya-ya!*' Spiros exclaimed, tugging Miranda along with him. 'Meet my young friend, Miranda. He bent to kiss an elderly woman on the cheek, and then straightened up, turning to Miranda. 'This is my grandmother,' he explained with obvious pride, 'and next to her Petros, my youngest son, with his wife and children…'

And so it went on, down the long table, and while Miranda smiled she couldn't help remembering her own family, and the wedge she had driven between herself and them.

'This is what happens when my family comes together,' Spiros explained expansively, extending his arms wide to encompass Miranda. 'Everyone enjoys themselves. And now you are a member of my family.' He struck his chest for emphasis. 'I insist you meet everyone. Come with me.' He tugged her along by the hand. 'I'm going to introduce you to one of my closest friends.'

There was no arguing with Spiros when he was in this mood. Miranda followed happily, and then her smile quickly died.

'Theo, meet Miranda. Miranda, I'd like you to meet Theo Savakis.'

'We've already met.' Theo spoke coolly as he rose from his seat to greet her.

'You two know each other?' Spiros hardly missed a beat. 'That's wonderful! Well, if you will excuse me, I must be getting back to the kitchen...'

Was Spiros's voice coming down a long dark tunnel, or was she going mad? It hardly mattered, because Spiros had vanished, and now there was just Theo Savakis standing in front of her. She couldn't see past him; she couldn't see round him; she couldn't see anything but him. She felt stranded and alone, and very angry with herself for the rush of confusion that had left her speechless. Her first impulse was to follow Spiros back to the kitchen. But why should she do that? Why not stay and make polite conversation for a few moments? Was she frightened of Theo Savakis?

He was waiting for her to say something, with that confident, somewhat amused expression tugging at his lips. Well, she wasn't going to make a fool of herself for his entertainment.

To give herself a chance to regroup, Miranda focussed on a button on Theo's shirt. The button was white, pearly white, and his shirt was very white too—unlike the sliver of toned flesh just visible beneath the placket. And what a wonderful warm, spicy scent...

'Won't you join us, Miranda?'

She jerked back to attention on hearing his voice, and was furious to feel her face reddening beneath his gaze.

'Lexis, make room for Miranda to sit down, will you?'

There were businessmen seated at the long table, several of them still dressed for the office, though they had shed their jackets and dispensed with their ties. Theo appeared to be freshly showered, and was wearing dark trousers with his crisp shirt, and Miranda noticed how waves of his thick, damp black hair caressed his neck. It made her heart lurch unexpectedly.

There was only one other woman at the table—the woman he had called Lexis. She was staring up at Miranda now, brows raised and contempt brewing in her luminous sapphire eyes. She didn't want to move along the bench, not for another woman, and certainly not for one whose face was crimson and whose clothes were spattered with grease stains.

'Don't worry, I wasn't going to stay,' Miranda explained. 'I have to go and help Spiros in the kitchen.'

It was a great excuse, but she hated herself for being such a coward. The look she was getting from Lexis didn't help. She schooled her face to make it expressionless. Lexis was slim, and blonde, and very beautiful. In fact, Lexis was about as close to perfection as it got...

'Lexis! Move!'

Miranda's eyes widened into golf balls. Was that how Theo Savakis spoke to his women? She was equally amazed to see how quickly Lexis got her rear end into gear.

'Miranda?'

Theo indicated that she should sit down in the space that had been made for her, but she didn't feel like joining his harem. 'Thank you, but I'm too busy to sit down.'

'Not too busy to share one drink with me, I hope?'

He made it sound as if it would be rude to refuse, and she was conscious of the other men watching the mini-drama unfold. She didn't want the responsibility of bringing the Savakis universe crashing down, thanks to some mistimed feminist stand. 'All right, but just one.'

As he gave her a mocking bow she took her place on the bench, sliding in beside Lexis, which was like sitting next to a wall of ice. Theo appeared not to notice. He appeared to be completely, infuriatingly relaxed.

'Spiros tells me you're going to sing for us tonight.'

He leaned towards her as he spoke, so that she had no place to look but into his eyes.

'That's right.' She felt as if she was being sucked down into some very complex shadows.

'Chef and cabaret singer? We had no idea your friend was so talented, Theo.'

Lexis's scorn-filled voice made Miranda's back stiffen, but she was careful not to show her feelings.

'How did you say you two met, Theo?' Lexis pressed.

'I didn't.'

If he had given an hour's explanation he couldn't have generated more interest around the table. And was that amusement tugging at his lips? Miranda looked away quickly as he straightened up.

'Gentlemen—and lady,' he announced with some ceremony, 'allow me to present Miranda—'

Miranda tensed, waiting for Theo to announce her full name, waiting for the questions that would inevitably follow—questions she didn't want to answer.

'I had the opportunity to see Miranda briefly in London once,' he said, with barely a pause, 'and then, by some incredible coincidence we met again on the beach this morning.'

'Incredible,' Lexis murmured. But her voice was lost in the

general buzz of interest. Lost to everyone, that was, except Miranda.

Miranda stared at Theo. Why had he lied about seeing her in London when they had never met before this morning? He held her gaze, as if willing her to say nothing, and she dipped her head minutely in gratitude at the way he had handled the situation.

'And now Miranda's here on Kalmos, working as a Jack-of-all-trades for your good friend Spiros?' Lexis observed. 'How convenient for you.'

Did Lexis think she was Theo's mistress? No, out of the question. So was *Lexis* Theo's mistress? Miranda was surprised at the force of her rejection of this thought. Why the hell should she care a fig for his domestic arrangements?

Raising the glass of wine Theo had poured for her, she tipped it in a toast.

'*Ya sou sas*, Miranda,' Theo responded, with a faintly curving smile. Everyone at the table but Lexis echoed his words.

'So, is this how you make your living?' Lexis said, opening her eyes a little wider.

This was no innocent enquiry, Miranda realised. Lexis's eyes were as bright as if she had a fever. The fever to stifle competition? 'If you mean do I work for a living,' she replied pleasantly, 'the answer is, yes, I do.'

'You're a busy woman, aren't you, Miranda?' Theo spoke in a relaxed manner, to dispel the tension that had brought a sudden hush to the table.

Was that barely perceptible sound—something like a cat snore—Lexis sniggering? Miranda wondered. She was still burning from her innuendoes.

'*Mezedes?*'

She collected herself as Theo offered her a plate loaded with delicacies.

'Thank you, Theo.' She was determined to stay now, determined to face it out, determined to keep her voice neutral. She was not going to let Lexis insinuate that she was a rich man's tart and get away with it.

Agalia's snacks lightened everyone spirits; they were delicious crispy filo pastry parcels filled with spinach and a soft, tangy cheese. But after a few moments Lexis said, 'Doesn't *that* make life hard for you?'

Miranda paused mid-munch. 'I'm sorry? What are you talking about?' And then she saw the curl of distaste on the other girl's lips as Lexis stared at her injuries. And now the men were looking too—except for Theo.

Perhaps because he wanted to distract everyone from Lexis's deliberate jibe, one of the older men said in an overly loud voice, 'I have a complaint to lodge with you, Theo.'

'Which is?' Theo demanded good-naturedly.

Miranda noticed how easily he smiled, even when he sensed a joke at his own expense coming along. The smile lit up his face…

'You always have the most beautiful women seated next to *you*.'

There was a chorus of agreement as the tension drained away, and Miranda suspected Lexis must be preening, flashing her perfect white smile.

'Well, you know what they say, Costas…'

Miranda held her breath, wondering what Theo was about to reveal.

'A beautiful woman is like a painting. Having one doesn't stop you wanting another.'

She almost choked on her pastry. Everyone else was laughing now, including Lexis. And Theo was staring at her with that same mocking challenge in his eyes. How had she ever thought him attractive? How had she ever come to relax her guard? She should have known Greek tycoons were hardly standard bearers for equality, but did this one have to be the worst type of alpha male?

Her cheeks were blazing. She couldn't bear to have complete strangers evaluating her—though Lexis seemed to take it in her stride, as if they were both on the open market.

She stood up abruptly.

'Miranda? Where are you going?'

She looked down coldly at Theo's hand, resting on her arm. 'Will you let me go, please? I've got work to do.' Why would he possibly want to keep her at the table—to humiliate her some more?

He stood too, shielding her from the rest of the table. 'Won't you stay a little longer?'

'No, thank you.'

'You don't appreciate my sense of humour?'

Her eyes were cold. 'I love it.' Moving past him, she smiled at the other men. 'I enjoyed meeting all of you.' Turning back to him, she said crisply, 'Thank you very much for the drink.'

'Must you go?' Lexis's query was loaded with sarcasm.

'I'd love to stay and chat with you, but as you know I have to sing.'

'Oh, yes.' Lexis sighed. 'We're *so* looking forward to that—aren't we, Theo?'

Theo didn't answer. In fact, he barely shrugged. His eyes were shuttered, and Miranda guessed he wasn't used to women walking out on him without permission.

Tough.

He might be gorgeous, but as far as she was concerned he was a patronising misogynist. Any man who collected women like so many works of art was an idiot. But as she went to move past he caught hold of her arm and swung her round.

'Do you do requests?'

'No, Theo, I don't. And this isn't a bell chain,' she added, glancing at her arm. 'If you want to ask me something, you don't have to jerk on my arm for attention. You only have to ask.'

'I may have to take you up on that.'

'Please don't,' she snapped.

'I've not made a great start, have I?' he said.

'A start to what?'

Slanting a gaze at her, he put his hand in front of his mouth and blew on his fingers as though they'd been burned. 'Angry lady.'

'Well, you've got something right tonight. Now, can I go?'

With an ironic wave of his arm, he moved aside to let her pass.

It had been hard, wriggling out of her casual clothes in the confined space Agalia had found for her with only one hand working properly, but somehow Miranda had shoehorned her way into the gown. It was a little bit of glamour: a ruby-red sheath, floor-length and fitted. And it was suitcase-friendly, in a crush-free fabric.

Freeing her hair, she combed it through with her fingers. Her face looked deathly white in the mirror Spiros had propped up for her on a shelf, and her eyes were huge and very green. When she shivered now it wasn't with cold—she was petrified. She didn't have an entourage to guard her back, as she'd had in the old days; tonight she was on her own.

Peeping through the curtain, she saw Theo had turned his chair around to face the improvised stage. Lexis was sitting beside him.

Forget Lexis. Did Theo Savakis have to have the sexiest mouth she had ever seen?

Okay, forget that too. Taking a deep breath, she walked into the spotlight.

CHAPTER THREE

THE first song went without a hitch and received enthusiastic applause. Perched on a barstool, Miranda found she was growing in confidence. She launched into a favourite late-night ballad in her trademark smoky voice.

The third song involved walking around the tables. Normally this wouldn't have concerned her, but she had underestimated the difficulty of removing the microphone from the stand with one hand out of action. By the time she freed the microphone she was uncharacteristically flustered, and with a clumsiness born of nerves she caught the heel of her shoe in her gown. As she stumbled, she heard a collective gasp, but the next thing she knew she was being held up by a pair of strong hands.

'This just isn't your night, is it?'

Theo had saved her from falling on her arm and almost certainly aggravating the injury, but close up he looked a lot more dangerous than he ever had before.

'Are you sure you're all right?'

The murmur reassured her; the private smile they exchanged she wasn't so sure about. 'No damage done,' she confirmed discreetly as he steadied her back on her feet.

She made a joke of it with the audience while Theo returned

to his seat, and soon had the good-natured crowd on her side. Only Lexis stared coldly at her, as if she would have much preferred her to stay down for the count. Lexis in her low-cut dress, with half a ton of diamonds weighing her down...

Let's face it, Theo would always have a beautiful woman on his arm. And Miranda had never felt the urge to be part of a crowd...

What was she thinking? Miranda averted her glance from Theo as he sat down. He was nothing to her. So why was her heart beating like a piston?

Closing her mind to everything but the music, she made sure that the rest of the set went without a hitch. But when Theo stood up to leave she was thrown again. She watched him drape a pashmina around Lexis's shoulders and had to force herself to concentrate as he ushered her out of the taverna.

Pausing by the door, Theo wondered if Miranda would notice he was leaving. But she was too absorbed in the music, denying him the chance to take another look into those incredible emerald eyes. She intrigued him and irritated him in equal part. He had never met a woman who was so vulnerable and yet so aggressive. And she was a great-looking woman too, with that fantastic night-dark hair and peachy skin.

Because he had known her in her former incarnation as a violinist he hadn't expected her to be such a good singer. Maybe she wasn't great in the true sense of the word, but she was certainly special: that husky voice and soulful delivery touched him somewhere deep. And that was a talent in itself. No one touched him. Ever.

No one, Theo reflected ironically as he helped Lexis into the car—and especially not his grandfather's choice of bride for him. Lexis was so far short of the mark it was a joke. Whatever Dimitri might have thought, Lexis was a wild child, the

Greek equivalent of an It Girl. She was already pining for the bubblegum generation. There wasn't enough excitement for Lexis in Kalmos—no clubs where she might get herself noticed, no paparazzi hanging round the door, no crazy surfers cosying up to her in need of a loan. He was going to do as she had asked and get her on the first flight home.

It jeopardised the agreement he had signed with Dimitri, of course. But maybe fate was smiling on him. Of course it made no sense in many ways—Miranda Weston was everything his grandfather had warned him against—but that in itself made her interesting.

The business could do without him for a while. Miranda Weston wasn't the only one who needed a holiday…

'We've put a sunbed and a parasol on the beach for you.'

'Spiros?' Pulling the receiver away from her mouth as she subdued a yawn, Miranda glanced at the clock. She had slept right through her alarm! 'I'm sorry, I must have overslept.'

Spiros's reaction was not the reaction of the average employer. His robust laugh forced Miranda to pull the receiver away from her ear again.

'You deserve to sleep in! This is just a little thank-you from Agalia and me for your wonderful performance last night. We want you to enjoy your stay while you're with us on Kalmos. It can't be all work, you know.'

'So you put a sunbed on the beach for me?' Slipping out of bed, Miranda padded across the cool tiled floor to take a look. 'Just a minute while I open the shutters… Oh, I see it!'

She sounded childlike; excited. Perhaps for once she would relax, and he could get to know her a little better, Theo mused, standing at his good friend's shoulder.

'Thank you, Spiros,' he said, clapping the older man on the shoulder. 'I'll see you later.'

Spiros gave him a shrewd stare. 'Something tells me we are going to be seeing a lot of you this visit, Theo.'

Pausing to smile, Theo slipped on his sunglasses again, and kept his thoughts to himself.

Miranda had no sooner settled into the comfortable cushions than she shot up again. The roar of the outboard engine was tuned to a certain key, like a song. Like a warning!

Her heart was thundering as she scanned the glittering surface of the sea, and when the boat came into view she quickly grabbed her wrap and started gathering all her clutter together.

'You're not running away from me, are you?'

She might have known Theo would beat the world record in transfers from boat to shore. 'No, I'm not running away from you,' she managed coolly, but it was a fight to keep her voice steady.

'Is this a private area?' He scanned the deserted beach. 'Or can anyone sit here?'

'Be my guest. I can't stop you.'

'How can I refuse such a charming invitation?'

At least he was wearing more clothes than the last time she had seen him on a boat, Miranda noticed with relief: frayed denim shorts, bleached almost white by the sun, with an old vest top. *Haute couture* for billionaires? She didn't think so. These were the genuine article, not some fancy make that had been treated to a fake distressed finish. He looked like a deckhand, rugged and toned, with wayward hair and a wicked line in smiles.

Lolling back with as much grace as she could muster, she slipped her dark glasses from their perch on top of her head and slowly lowered them onto her nose. 'Why are you here, Theo?'

'Why? To see you, of course.'

Theo hunkered down so their faces were on a level. She

turned her head to look at him and he could see the pulse beating in her neck—her *racing* pulse, fluttering in her neck. He had to govern every one of his reactions, using every trick in the book to keep her from suspecting the effect that was having on him. 'Did I hurt you when I grabbed your arm last night?'

'Only my pride.'

'Well, I'm sorry. I hope you accept my apology?' He was relieved when she inclined her head a fraction. 'I forgot. About your arm, I mean.'

She didn't look convinced. And now she looked uncomfortable. Maybe she thought he shouldn't have broached the topic, but someone had to. 'I don't see you that way, Miranda,' he said quietly.

'What do you mean?'

She had tensed visibly. 'I don't see you in terms of your injury,' he explained. 'That's why I forgot about it.'

'So you weren't just careless?'

'I wanted to speak to you, not your arm.'

Better. She almost smiled. He could see her fighting to hold it in. 'I was at your first concert at the Royal Albert Hall in London. I heard you perform.'

'Oh! Oh, I see.'

'You thought I was lying about seeing you in London?'

'Well, I…'

Of course she had. She made a dismissive gesture, but he could see he had surprised her.

'You must have seen me on my first and last concert tour.'

And now she was off in her own world somewhere. 'So the accident happened while you were in London?'

As he asked the question her desperation for him to change the subject lit up in neon lights. He could never have anticipated that it would have such a bad effect on her. After all, how long had it been—months now, surely? What was she hiding? She wasn't going to tell him now.

He looked at the sky, seeking distraction in the weather. 'The sun gets to everyone in the end. I can see you're in no mood for talking.'

'I am,' she disagreed. And then after a moment she added, 'You still haven't told me why you wanted to see me.'

'I've come to ask you to a party on my yacht tonight.'

He reeled back as she jerked into a sitting position.

'What? As your performing monkey? Or are you short of waitresses, Theo?'

'Neither.' He stood up to put some distance between them. 'I'm inviting you to the party as my guest.'

Slipping her sunglasses down her nose, she gave him a long, considering look—as if she was weighing him up to see whether or not he could be trusted.

'As your guest?'

'That's what I said.'

He watched her drop her sunglasses again and gaze out across the bay at the sleek white colossus he had always thought of as a toy…a toy to entice, as well as a toy for his own enjoyment. He could usually detect a flare behind the eyes when he issued an invitation like this—of anticipation, of excitement. But Miranda wasn't so easy to fathom. After her meteoric rise to the very zenith of her profession she had experienced so many things. Would a party on board a luxury yacht only serve as a reminder to her of everything she had lost?

Lowering her sunglasses to the tip of her nose, she answered his question.

'Thank you, Theo. I'd like that.'

He should have known she would show more character. And there were no fireworks, no acquisitive gleam in her eyes. The only fireworks going off were inside him. 'Good. Why don't you come along with Spiros and Agalia?'

'They're coming?'

As he'd hoped, that relaxed her completely. He wanted to be sure she felt comfortable from the moment she arrived. 'They're invited.' He gave a shrug, as casual as he could make it. 'I'll send a boat for you.'

'See you tonight, then,' she said.

She didn't turn her head towards him as she spoke. He liked that. She was as cool as he was, which had the effect of making him doubly hot for her.

Miranda's outfit was a compromise. She told herself it was simple, but effective.

Amazing how you could convince yourself of anything when you wanted to, Miranda mused as she stared at herself in the full-length mirror in her bedroom at the apartment. She was wearing cropped black pants with plain black sandals—no one would be wearing high heels on an expensive teak deck. So far, so good. She had teamed these with a white strappy top to show off the first hint of a suntan, and had left her hair loose because it made her feel sexy that way. And, yes, okay, because she did want Theo to notice her. And then, because she was still conscious of her scars, no matter how many times she reminded herself that Theo had said they were irrelevant, she added her one and only shawl to the mix, draping it around her shoulders so that it covered her injuries.

Spiros and Agalia were right on time, but Agalia seemed agitated, and Miranda soon discovered why.

'Theo sent a powerboat for us, but Spiros sent it away. He insists on rowing us out to the yacht,' Agalia explained, plucking at a button on the front of her dress.

'It will be lovely out on the water tonight,' Spiros said, looking to Miranda for support.

'Yes, but we want to arrive before the party is over, Spiros,' Agalia pointed out.

'I'm happy whatever we do,' Miranda said, smiling at both of them. 'Really, Agalia, don't worry—this is fine by me.'

But it wasn't fine. In fact it was extremely wet. Within yards of the shore the wind kicked up, and all of them were drenched.

Miranda and Agalia clung onto the sides as Spiros flung his back into his rowing in an attempt to beat the waves threatening to swamp the small boat. Progress was painfully slow, but finally Spiros brought them under the lee of Theo's yacht.

Shielded from the worst of the wind, it was still a tricky manoeuvre to keep the rowing boat in place while they climbed on board. Fortunately, some crew had been watching their progress with concern, and quickly came down the steel ladder to lash the small craft to the stern.

As they threw a blanket round her shoulders, Miranda could see the strings of lights criss-crossing the prow and midships, where the party was being held. A live band was playing, and it was clear the short-lived squall hadn't dampened anyone's enthusiasm. From the sound of it, she gathered it was a large party. She felt reassured, knowing she wouldn't be subjected to scrutiny when she finally made an appearance. She could always lose herself in a crowd.

Thanks to the party being in full swing their arrival had largely gone unnoticed, which was a bonus. At least there would be chance to dry off and recover before she had to face Theo. But Miranda could see that Agalia was angry, and that Spiros's pride had been badly dented. She hurried to reassure them and make a joke of their drenching. Far from being sophisticated guests at a glamorous party, they looked more like three drowned rats.

At last Agalia's face cracked and she saw the funny side of it, and by the time a crew member rushed up to escort them below decks, where they could take a shower and recover, all three of them were laughing helplessly.

'This is not quite the arrival I had planned for you,' Spiros admitted anxiously, chewing the tip of his moustache.

'No harm done, and we'll soon dry off,' Miranda assured him.

They were assigned staterooms where they could relax in comfortable robes after their showers while their clothes were being cleaned and dried for them. They agreed to wait for each other, and to make their appearance as a united team.

'Shipmates?' Miranda suggested.

'Lunatics,' Agalia argued, whacking Spiros affectionately over the head with her wet shawl.

CHAPTER FOUR

BY the time the knock came on the cabin door Miranda's eyes had been opened to what it meant to live a life where expense was no object. Banks of snowy white towels stretched to the ceiling in the bathroom, which was of course lined in marble, with all the latest in high-tech fittings. There was even a flatscreen TV on the wall for those idle moments in the bath, not to mention an invisible sound system. In the stateroom itself there were priceless *objets d'art* from right across the globe, and the type of sumptuous fabrics to which the damning label 'manmade' could never be attached. In fact, everywhere she looked everything was of the best.

'I could get used to this very quickly,' she said to herself, padding across to answer the door in a warm, plush robe. 'In fact, I feel like a princess.' She opened the door and smiled at the uniformed steward who stood there.

'Here's your uniform. Hurry up, they're waiting for you in the galley. And don't forget to tie your hair back.'

Miranda's jaw dropped. Her reign as a princess had been somewhat short-lived! Her mouth was still open when the steward had disappeared down the corridor. Flattening her lips, she pressed them together angrily. She should have known. Why had she fallen for it? Had she thought a leopard like Theo Savakis could change his spots in the space of a day?

When Miranda finally emerged from the stateroom Spiros and Agalia were waiting for her outside their own room.

'What on earth are you wearing, Miranda?' Agalia said, staring at the smart black dress and white apron. 'What happened to your clothes?'

'They were taken away, I suppose. These were just delivered.'

'But you can't go up on deck dressed like that. Someone will ask you to get them a drink!'

Spiros's eyes were twinkling, but Agalia soon put him right with a hissing sound and a firm hand on his arm. 'This isn't funny, Spiros.'

'Oh, I see… No, I suppose not,' he said, realising his mistake. 'So what will you wear, Miranda?'

'Why, this of course.' There was steel in Miranda's voice, and the glint of battle in her eyes. If this was someone's idea of a joke, she was about to call their bluff.

'You're not serious?' Agalia was quite clearly horrorstruck.

'Oh, but I am,' Miranda said evenly. 'Don't worry about me. I'm a big girl now. Really,' she added, seeing her two friends exchange a glance, 'I'll be fine.'

Miranda felt Theo's presence on deck before she could see him. And then she spotted him, standing in the centre of an admiring throng with Lexis hovering just on periphery of the group. She felt sure Lexis was in on it, because she kept spearing glances at the companionway leading to the guest suites.

Lexis knew what to expect, all right—but had Theo put her up to it?

With aplomb, Miranda removed a tray from the hands of a passing waiter. 'Don't worry,' she reassured him. 'The weather delayed me, but when I arrived they told me to take care of the drinks.'

He looked at her uncertainly for a moment, and then backed off. Fully armed, she made straight for his boss.

Theo turned immediately. 'Miranda! They told me you had arrived. Thank goodness you're all right! Did they look after you properly? I would have come to see you myself, but there were so many guests…'

'Don't worry, Theo, I can imagine how busy you must have been.'

'Miranda?' Her sarcasm stalled him, and for the first time he looked her over properly. 'What are you wearing? This isn't a fancy dress party, you know.'

'Yes, I do know that, Theo. These are the clothes that were sent to the stateroom for me to wear.'

'Don't be ridiculous.'

'I don't think *I'm* the one being foolish here, Theo.'

Without breaking his stare, he barely had to crook his little finger for the same waiter she had swiped the tray from to reappear.

'Take this tray from Miss Weston, will you? And have someone find Miss Weston's clothes. I believe they're being cleaned and dried out, so you might start in the laundry room.'

'The laundry room? I'm impressed,' she said stonily.

'Then you impress far too easily.' There was a glint in Theo's eyes.

'So you're not responsible for sending this uniform to my stateroom?'

'What do you think, Miranda? I'll be in my suite,' he added to the steward.

'What do you think you're doing?' Miranda could feel Lexis's gaze boring into her back as Theo took a firm hold of her arm and steered her towards another flight of steps.

'We'll talk when we get there.'

'No, we'll talk now.' Stopping dead at the top of them,

Miranda firmed her jaw. 'As far as I know, I'm not hanging on your wall just yet.'

'Meaning?'

'Remember those paintings you were bragging about, Theo? Well, I'm not one of them. And I'm not going anywhere with you until you tell me what all this is about.'

'All what?'

She pointed to her outfit. 'Will there be another set of clothes delivered to my stateroom later on, for when I have to sing to your guests?'

'I'm disappointed in you, Miranda, if that's what you think of me.'

She drew an angry breath and mulled it over for a moment. Truthfully, she couldn't picture Theo wasting his time on such a clumsy put-down. 'You didn't pull this stunt, did you?'

Theo levelled a stare on her face, brow raised, eyes amused.

'So, who did, then?' Miranda tried to ignore the fact that her heart was thundering.

'I think we both know the answer to that.' Theo gazed down the deck to where Lexis was dirty-dancing in the shadows with another young guest.

'But I thought you and—'

'Me and Lexis?' Theo cut across her. 'Not this side of sanity, Miranda, I can assure you.'

'But you both seem…'

'To know each other? We do. Lexis is the daughter of another shipping family.'

'Oh. I see.'

Switching the clothes must have been Lexis's infantile idea of a joke, Theo guessed. He wanted to reassure Miranda that the other girl held no appeal for him, and was relieved when he saw a faint smile on her lips.

'I found it hard to believe that it was you,' she admitted.

He smiled, easing his shoulders in a shrug. 'Please accept my apologies anyway.'

'I do.'

'But why would Lexis do a thing like that? Why feel the need to be so unpleasant?'

'Because she knows I don't want her, and she sees you as competition.'

'Me?' She looked incredulous. 'Oh, come on.'

He had to be careful what he said. Miranda didn't see herself as beautiful...which said *what* about his feelings towards her? It might be an idea to find out. 'Can I offer you a drink while we wait for your clothes to arrive?' When she looked back towards the party he found himself adding, 'In my stateroom. I'll make sure they call me there.'

Theo's lips were curving in a way Miranda wished she didn't find quite so attractive, and his eyes were clear and frank. 'Well, I...' But then she remembered that he wasn't always quite so uncomplicated. 'I'm not sure I should.'

'And why is that?'

'Should I go to a man's stateroom when he admits that he views women as so many works of art? I'm not sure I want to be considered as a possible collectable.'

It surprised him to feel a rush of satisfaction seeing her confidence had returned to the point where she would challenge him. 'You're right to be cautious. But I should tell you that my collection is priceless.'

Women or paintings? Miranda wondered. And then she realised that she was dangerously close to flirting with him, and cooled her expression.

'Are you coming or not?' Theo pressed. 'I thought you wanted to get out of those clothes?'

'I do.'

'Then come with me. I can assure you my crew will find yours and bring them to us there.'

He gestured towards the shadows pooling at the bottom of the companionway, but as he sought to reassure her Miranda's mind was racing. Why wouldn't Theo remain on deck to mingle with his guests? Why couldn't one of the stewards tell her when her clothes had been found? But of course as a considerate host it was his duty to make sure everything turned out all right after the way she had been treated...

'Although that *is* a very fetching outfit,' he observed, reclaiming her attention. 'The Peter Pan collar is a particularly nice touch.'

'Well, I feel ridiculous!'

'I can assure you that you don't look the least bit ridiculous to me.' And now he'd said too much. He stepped back, putting some distance between them. She was still uncertain, and the last thing he wanted was to move too fast.

'What if they can't be found?'

As she turned her face up to him he felt his heart thud heavily in his chest. This was extraordinary, this feeling inside him...but not unpleasant. 'If the worst happens I'm sure we'll find you something else to wear.'

'A negligee? A French maid's outfit?'

She wasn't ready for this, Miranda realised as he smiled devastatingly. Flirting with Theo Savakis was out of her league. But then she saw Agalia and Spiros and they were giving her an encouraging nod. They had been on their way over to talk to her and had halted mid-step, realising who she was talking to. Surely they wouldn't send her below decks with a man they considered dangerous? And, as Theo had pointed out earlier, she couldn't stay at the party wearing fancy dress. 'All right,' she agreed finally.

* * *

Miranda's pulse gathered speed as she gazed around Theo's fabulous stateroom. It was about three times the size of the one she had been allocated. But she had to ask herself—what was she doing alone with him?

'I'm going to call and see what progress has been made,' he said. 'And in the meantime...' He gazed at her as he punched in some numbers on the phone. 'I can only apologise for the inconvenience you have experienced so far this evening.'

'Thank you. You're a very considerate host.'

'And you're too kind.' He pulled a wry smile, and then turned to fire off some words in Greek. 'Now we wait. Don't look so worried. I can assure you I don't bite. Won't you sit down?'

She headed for a straight-backed chair, stiff and uncomfortable.

'You'd be better on the sofa.'

'I'm fine here,' she assured him, perching on the edge of her seat.

'We didn't get off to the best of starts,' he commented ruefully. 'I had hoped that this evening would make up for it.'

'Don't worry, it can only get better.' Now, why had she felt the need to reassure him?

They both turned at a knock on the door. But rather than her clothes it was a waiter, with a tray of champagne and some scrumptious-looking canapés.

'The evening hasn't been much fun for you up to now,' Theo explained, 'and I didn't see why you should have to miss the party. Champagne?'

She hesitated, wondering if he had planned it this way. 'How long do you think my clothes will take?'

'As long as it takes you to drink one glass of champagne.'

His smile was infectious. 'And if I drink quickly?'

'Two.'

Theo was looking at her in a way that made it impossible to think the worst of him. 'Okay, I'd love a glass.'

'Feel free to remove your apron.'

'What? Oh!' She laughed easily for the first time. Life looked so much better through a cloud of champagne bubbles.

'Another glass?' Theo suggested, before she got round to the apron.

Why not? She wasn't used to drinking, and was still a bit edgy. Time was ticking by with no sign of her clothes. She had downed the first glass of champagne in a thirsty gulp, and the second slipped down just as easily. She was a little unsteady on her feet by the time she stood up to sort out the ties at her back. 'Is this boat moving?'

Theo was at her side in an instant, with a steadying hand beneath her arm. 'I'll order some orange juice,' he said, deftly freeing the knot at the back of her waist.

'Perhaps black coffee would be better...' Theo's face seemed very close as she stared up at him. 'Lots of it, and strong.' She wasn't prepared for him capturing a tendril of her hair to wind around his finger. 'Theo...'

'Miranda...'

He said her name in a teasing way, and she wasn't sure if Theo drew her closer or if she swayed towards him. She only knew that their mouths were almost touching, and that her lips were tingling, and that she was happy to drown in the scent of sandalwood and clean warm man. 'What's happening to me?'

'I would have thought that was obvious...'

She frowned and pulled back a step. 'Why are you whispering? Why am I?' She shook her head. 'And why am I flirting with you?'

'I don't know, but you're very good at it. Shall I kiss you, Miranda? Would you like that?'

Her body certainly seemed to think he should.

'Let me put it another way—would you rather I didn't?'

'Oh, no, no—that would be fine.' She closed her eyes and waited.

Nothing.

She opened her eyes again indignantly. 'Do you enjoy teasing me?' she demanded, firming her mouth as far as her traitorous lips would allow.

'Very much,' he admitted softly.

'Did you plan this?'

'Hand on my heart, no.' Just a fortunate coincidence, Theo reflected, trying to remember the last time he had owed any thanks to a short-lived storm.

'All right, I forgive you.' Miranda's jade-green gaze flicked up.

Theo drew her into his arms and kissed her chastely on the lips.

Chastely, yes, but he knew exactly what he was doing, Miranda realised as her body yearned towards him.

'Better?' he murmured.

She heard the humour in his voice and ignored it. 'Absolutely not.'

Had she really believed the accident had drained all the passion from her life? Nothing had ever fired her like her lost talent for making music—nothing until just now, when Theo had kissed her. So was this wild frenzy in her mind, this all-pervading sense of rightness, of love? Or was she going crazy? Her body was melting, craving, aching. Had she really put all thoughts of sex out of her life after one failed attempt? Right now she could think of nothing else...

When Theo kissed her again he made it slow, seductively slipping his tongue between her teeth to taste her and then pulling back the moment she softened against him.

Nipping the full swell of her bottom lip, he smiled against her mouth.

'Is this what you want, Miranda?' he murmured, rasping the stubble on his chin against the most sensitive part of her neck.

'No, I don't…' But her sigh told him otherwise, and as she gazed into his eyes—such dark, beautiful eyes—she wanted nothing more than for Theo to hold her.

'Well, this is exactly what I want,' he said.

And then she could only quiver beneath his touch as he feathered strokes down her spine. But when she tried to move closer he pulled back.

'No, Miranda.'

'No?' Miranda's face reddened as she stared up. She couldn't even catch her breath, but Theo was perfectly calm.

'I'm not going to make love to you here, while we're waiting for a steward to arrive with your clothes.'

'Too right,' she snapped, caught in a maelstrom of emotion and desire, and she swung away. Teasing was one thing, but this had gone too far.

Theo caught up with her at the door and gently pulled her back into his arms, holding her until she cautiously relaxed, and when she did it was the most wonderful and overwhelming feeling.

The idea had been growing on him steadily, and now he was sure. He had found his bride. He still had to convince her to marry him, of course.

It was an incredible stroke of good fortune that had brought Miranda to Kalmos. He needed a wife, but feeling as he did about her was a bonus he hadn't expected. Her obvious inexperience made him feel fiercely protective; he looked at her and felt…

The emotions he felt were new to him, and he didn't quite trust them. Therefore he used his business brain to analyse the positives and negatives. She was talented, she was beautiful, and from what he remembered her sister had married a prince. She didn't hesitate to stand up to him, which meant she was likely to keep his interest long-term. Genetically she was clearly sound, and any children they had would benefit from both gene pools. They wanted each other; that much was glaringly obvious. It was blindingly simple, really: this just felt right.

Slowly and carefully he relaxed his grip and let her go. 'You're very special, Miranda, and I want to see you again.'

It pleased him to exercise self-control, but if Miranda agreed to be his bride they would have to be married quickly—and not just for the sake of Dimitri's failing health. He had never found himself in this position before, knowing that no amount of mental control would be enough to subdue the physical desire raging through him. But then, for reasons that completely eluded him, he had never before wanted a woman as he wanted Miranda Weston.

He moved away from the door so that she could see all she had to do was walk past him and leave if she wanted to. She was still quite wary after what had happened between them, still not quite sure of him.

'Go up on deck to get a breath of fresh air if you want to, Miranda. I'll make sure someone comes to tell you the moment your clothes have been found.'

'No,' she said, as if she had come to a decision. 'I'll stay here.'

He felt a rush of triumph as she walked back into the room, and another when she chose the sofa. But as she turned to look at him he briefly felt a twinge of guilt. She'd had a lot to deal with since the accident—it had wrecked her life and she must still be haunted by it. Was it fair to marry a woman like Miranda when he didn't even know if he was capable of love? He didn't have any shining examples of happy family life to draw upon—and didn't she have enough baggage to carry around without him piling more regrets on top of those she had already accumulated?

Dimitri said that when you shut out emotion your journey through life was easy. He had grown up believing Dimitri was right. Even as a child love had seemed to him like an unattainable goal, secretly desired but always denied. As an adult he had learned not to expect it. Letting down the barricades only led to disappointment.

Theo pulled himself together, rejoicing in the fact that, as it always did, logic had saved him. He needed a bride; Miranda needed a protector to care for her while she recovered from her injuries and forged a new life. If she agreed to marry him he would give her the world. In return for the bargain they would forge he would protect her. And love would come from the children they had together.

CHAPTER FIVE

'I ATTENDED one of your concerts, Miranda, and you had me hooked,' Theo remarked, deliberately changing the mood.

'Do you have my CD?'

'Of the Brahms? No, I don't.'

Her frankness had thrown him for a moment, but he wasn't going to lie to her. That was Miranda, he was fast discovering. Always to the point. The type of woman he was used to would have covered for him. Not Miranda. She cut right through the bull, exposing any tiny bit of flattery for what it was: a means to an end. Every flatterer had something to gain. Her career might have been short, but she had learned that lesson. He toned it down. 'I'm not even that keen on violin concertos, but hearing you play—'

'Can we talk about something else, please, Theo?' She cut across him, clearly unimpressed. 'Surely we can find some other common ground?'

'Of course we can.' He searched for something else to discuss, and for once in his life nothing came to him. It was a first. Whether in business or at a social function he was always sure-footed, always confident. He'd have to come up with some new rules of conduct for courting a prospective wife—and fast.

'What's in it for you, Theo?'

He sharpened his focus. 'What are you talking about?' he said carefully.

'Being so nice to me.'

What could he say? He had wanted to make love to her and had then decided that he had more to gain from marrying her? He could hardly tell her what lay behind his interest.

He let out his breath slowly. 'Does there have to be something in it for me?' Tipping his head, he viewed her keenly, and got a direct stare right back. 'Okay.' He held up his hands in mock surrender. 'You're right. I'm usually a better host than this. I let you down tonight and I'm trying to make up for it.'

There was a knock on the door, and when he called out a maid entered with Miranda's neatly pressed clothes in her arms. Although it had been a prolonged wait, rather than complaining he felt like falling on his knees and praising his staff for giving him space. 'Thank you.' Taking them from the maid, he closed the door and turned to Miranda. 'Use my bedroom—or the bathroom, if you prefer.'

Holding the outfit up, she exclaimed, 'They're as good as new. I'm impressed!'

At last, a result! And then he discovered that it pleased him to please her. It pleased him even more to see her smiling and relaxed, because that meant he was one step further forward and they could both relax.

'You're a very lucky man, Theo.'

Wisely, he said nothing.

'I won't be long.' With a fleeting smile, she made for one of the doors he had indicated.

She was almost as good as her word. He only had time to pace round the salon three times before she returned.

'You look lovely,' he murmured. Major understatement.

With her hair loose, the understated outfit, and no adornment other than her sun-kissed skin, she looked sensational.

'Are you ready for the party?' He offered to link arms.

She hesitated for a moment. It was the longest moment of his life.

'Okay.' She flashed him a smile and walked forward to take his arm. 'Let's do it.'

Briefly her trust brought on the guilt again. Why did he have to trap someone so pure and lovely in a web of business strategy? But the business had to be saved. Fortunately for him Miranda was an intelligent woman, and he was confident that she would soon come to see the long-term benefits of his plan. The red-hot attraction between them would make it easier for both of them.

She hadn't known it was possible to have so much fun with a man. When he relaxed, Theo was the best of company. By the end of the evening Miranda was beginning to conclude that she had misjudged him. She had certainly been a little harsh. Even Lexis didn't seem to mind that she was dancing with him. But then Lexis was enjoying herself with a high-spirited group much closer to her own age.

Theo made a point of introducing her to his friends—charming people, some of whom even remembered her starburst career but were sensitive enough not to probe. She could get used to this, Miranda realised, smiling happily, but she also had to remember she was going home soon, and to a very different life.

'Is this a Greek thing?' she found a chance to ask him during a lull in the conversation.

'A Greek thing?' Theo frowned as he leaned closer to hear her over the music and chatter.

Only Theo could smile and frown at the same time, Miranda

thought, feeling her senses stir as she looked at him. 'I mean all the *bonhomie*. It cuts right across every barrier—'

'*Bonhomie?*' He smiled down at her. 'I thought that was a French thing?'

When he teased her in that confidential tone, and leaned close enough for her to feel the sweep of his warm, minty breath, it was impossible to concentrate. 'You know what I'm talking about, Theo,' she chastised him gently. 'Everyone mixes so easily here in Greece.'

'Everyone?' Pulling back, he gazed around. 'We're all the same at heart—surely that's the only thing that matters?'

'Well, I love being part of it.'

'You do?'

She had been too frank—but what the hell? 'Yes, I do.'

'In that case, I've got another suggestion for you.' Taking her arm, he led her to the bow rail, where it was quieter and they could have a little privacy. 'Come swimming with me to-morrow.' He drew her in front of him. 'No strings, no company. Just you, me, and a very private beach…'

'Just you and me?'

He saw the flicker of concern in her eyes and knew he should reassure her, even if he did have rather more style than she seemed to imagine—grinding skin against sand had never been his sexual position of choice. 'You, me…and Agalia as chaperone.'

'Really?'

His suggestion was working. She gave him what he thought of as her funny stare: half-grin, but deadly serious behind the eyes. 'Yes, really.' He pressed his lips down in a wry smile. 'Why shouldn't we invite Agalia? It will be fun for her too.' That swung it. He didn't even wait for Miranda to say she agreed to his idea. 'Great. I'll pick you up at the apartment tomorrow morning at ten.'

'I'll look forward to it.'

He felt like punching the air when she smiled back at him. He had never felt like this before, not even when he'd signed his biggest deal...except, of course, that *this* was the biggest deal. 'That's great, Miranda,' he said, and kept his voice cool.

Agalia took her job as official chaperone so seriously that she arrived at Miranda's apartment shortly after nine to supervise her charge's preparations.

'You will take a shirt to cover up all that nakedness,' she insisted sternly.

Miranda had chosen the most modest costume in her small collection, but she suspected Agalia would have preferred her to don a Victorian bathing suit with matching mob cap. There was only one thing to do. She plundered the sparsely filled rail inside the simple wooden wardrobe, plucking out her comfiest shirt. It was a cover-all, with no sex appeal whatever: a brushed cotton faded plum number about ten sizes too large.

Agalia's face lit up when she saw it. 'Perfect. And you will need this too.'

'A book?' Miranda stared at the heavy, worthy-looking tome Agalia was holding out to her.

'It wasn't easy to find one in English,' Agalia told her, her mouth firming into a 'no surrender' line. 'It is just what you will need when you are sitting quietly in the shade. I have my own collection of books...' Opening her straw basket, she let Miranda peer inside to see a number of well-thumbed paperbacks.

'It's very good of you to go to all this trouble for me, Agalia.'

'Nonsense. How can you go out alone with a man on his boat unless I am with you? And what will you do when you reach the shore if you do not have a book to read?'

Miranda smothered her smile. When two worlds collided

it was better to respect the mores of the host country. Kalmos was tiny, and little changed, she suspected, for centuries. And far from resenting Agalia's attention, she felt as if the elderly Greek woman was standing in for her own mother.

It wasn't that she was a child again, but since the accident she hadn't been so sure of her own judgement...

Theo glanced at his wristwatch again. He was growing impatient. He'd arrived early, and the boat had been moored at the quayside for almost half an hour.

This was the most bizarre situation in which he had ever found himself. Having broken free from all those traditions that irked him, courting a woman in the old-fashioned way was hardly his area of expertise. But if that was what it took...

Here she was, and her eyes were fixed on what he held out to her.

'Flowers?' she exclaimed.

He watched Miranda gaze at the bouquet in his outstretched hand. They looked as if they had come from someone's garden and been carefully arranged before being simply tied at the base with a pale raffia band.

'Oh, Theo! They're absolutely beautiful...'

As she looked up at him her incredible jade-green eyes told him all he needed to know. Their expression was eloquent with surprise and delight.

'Thank you,' she said, taking them from him carefully.

'My pleasure.' He breathed a sigh of relief. Having simple flowers like this flown in from Athens was possibly the most extravagant gesture he had ever made.

'I'll just put them in water.'

She was still smiling when she turned away. It gave him quite a rush. He would normally have been feeling pretty pleased with himself, though for very different reasons. The flowers would have been a single step in a process both participants understood: a process conducted at a pace of his choosing that would lead to the inevitable conclusion in bed. But he had to remember that Miranda was inexperienced, and would therefore be unaware of such devices. Wooing the woman he intended to make his wife was very different from the norm; it required a lot more finesse. Hence the presence of Agalia, and his neatly groomed hair, the white polo shirt and respectable fawn Bermudas. He looked smooth and collected, but underneath he was humming with testosterone. He couldn't help it; that was just the way he was.

'Do you have things for me to carry?' The need to inhale Miranda's fresh, clean scent was starting to get to him.

He was right behind her. She could feel his gaze shimmering down her spine. 'Yes, all my things are over there...' She pointed vaguely. She didn't want to risk looking into his eyes, because there was something so seductive in his smile she didn't know if she could hide her feelings. 'And...' Her mouth dried as at last they locked glances.

'And?' Theo prompted her softly.

'There's Agalia's basket to carry,' she managed faintly.

Theo's 'boat' was a forty-foot sun-seeker's delight.

'I'm using this because one person can handle it and because it has a shallow draft,' he explained. 'The beach I'm taking you to is so secluded it can only be accessed from the sea. The sea at that point is very shallow, so—'

'You dipped into your lucky-bag of boats and came up with this one?' Miranda suggested dryly, coming to sit alongside him in the cockpit.

'Something like that.'

As Theo turned to gaze at her Miranda felt her breath catch in her throat. She quickly looked away, pretending interest in the scenery instead, which was beautiful. But she wasn't fooling anyone—even her earlobes were tingling.

Theo and Miranda waded ashore with the picnic, and then Theo returned to the boat to carry Agalia—as if she were thistledown, Miranda noticed, watching from the shade of a rustling tamarisk tree.

The tremor of alarm she felt at this practical demonstration of Theo's strength made an uncomfortable bedfellow for the frisson of arousal it provoked. All she could remember of sex was that it had hurt and left her feeling violated, and though she wanted Theo she found it impossible to shake off that first painful memory. But, watching Agalia laughing in his arms as he carried her so carefully, she did have to concede Theo had more control over his power than most men, and by the time he had reached the shallows her panic had subsided.

Agalia remained in the shade, lost in her novel, while Miranda and Theo lay at the edge of the surf chatting easily. When the sun grew too hot they retreated to a rockpool in the shade.

'The Greek islands provide sanctuary for more than one hundred species of orchid, thanks to the land having escaped the ravages of chemical fertilisers...'

Theo could have been telling her anything, Miranda thought as she struggled to concentrate. As a musician she had always been fascinated by beautiful sounds, and Theo's rich baritone voice was extremely beautiful...

'So, although the land is poor, there are undoubted benefits—' He broke off. 'You'll have to forgive me, Miranda, but conservation is one of my passions.'

Miranda was jolted back to attention. 'No, go on—I'm absolutely fascinated.' She wanted him to continue talking so that she had an excuse to stare at him. And the fact that he cared so deeply for such things was a both a revelation and a delight. He was full of surprises, and the more she found out about him, the more she wanted to find out about him.

They ate their picnic sitting together on a plaid blanket. The tartan seemed incongruous until Agalia pointed out that the Highlands of Scotland were just one of Theo's favourite haunts. The day had given her the opportunity to find out so much about him, Miranda realised, and she liked everything she had learned. Liking someone added a very powerful dimension to physical attraction. And how could she not be physically attracted to Theo?

She was the very model of reserve, in deference to Agalia, but the truth behind old-fashioned courtship was more startling than Miranda had realised. The sexual tension was extraordinary. The briefest glance, the faintest smile, the smallest gesture—each of them took on enormous significance. She wondered if Theo felt it too. And when Agalia fell asleep in the shade that question was answered.

As Agalia's breathing took on the rhythm of the surf Miranda turned her face to the sky. Closing her eyes, she leaned back on her hands, sighing with contentment. At first she wondered if she was dreaming, or if Theo's fingertips really were touching her own. It was only the lightest touch, but surely it was the most sensuous contact possible? When he trailed his fingertips across the back of her hand she gasped as a pulse of arousal took her by surprise.

Opening her eyes, she stared at him. Putting a finger over his lips, he tilted his head, indicating that she should follow him. Soundlessly, she got up and walked in his wake across the sand.

At one side of the cove the sea frothed and bubbled across some low-lying rocks. They were flat and slippery, and she was relieved when Theo reached out his hand to help her across them. He kept hold of her hand as they walked on around the curving cliff base. This led to a sandy inlet Miranda guessed must have been formed by centuries of waves stealing slivers from the shore.

They didn't speak, but she had never felt closer to anyone in her life. And when he came to a halt and drew her into his arms she didn't resist.

Kissing Theo was like sinking into someone and becoming them, becoming one, and when he finally pulled away to rest his forehead against her brow she saw that he was smiling too, as if they had both shared the same soaring emotion.

'I'm not going to let you go,' he whispered.

'I'm glad.'

'I don't think you understand me.'

'Oh?' Tilting up her chin, she stared at him, waiting for an explanation.

'I can't let you leave Kalmos until I'm sure you'll come back to me.'

'But I'm here for another week—'

'I'm not talking in terms of weeks, Miranda.'

'Then what do you mean?' She could hardly breathe, her heart was beating so rapidly. This was crazy. Surely he wasn't going to ask her to stay?

Taking hold of her hands very gently in his, he kissed each of her fingertips in turn, damaged and undamaged alike, and then the palm of each hand. 'We've known each other such a short time, and yet I feel I've known you for ever, Miranda. I don't want to lose you. I *won't* lose you.'

She could see he was engaged in some inner struggle that didn't allow him to meet her gaze. 'Lose me, Theo? I'm not going anywhere just yet—'

'Ever.'

'Ever?' She stared at him questioningly.

'Will you marry me, Miranda?'

'What?' she breathed incredulously.

'I said, will you marry me?'

Shaking her head, she tried in vain to form some sort of response, but she could only manage, 'But we hardly know each other.'

'We have a lifetime in front of us.'

'But we've only just met! You can't possibly know that you want to marry me!'

But he did. And there wasn't time for a long-drawn-out courtship. 'You'll be leaving Kalmos in a few short days, and I know what I want. I know what I've been waiting for. The only question is how do you feel, Miranda? Do you feel the same?'

'Shouldn't we talk about it first, at least?'

Allow her to ask questions he might have to refuse to answer? 'Yes—or no?' he said flatly, wishing it could be different when he saw the longing in her eyes. He consciously softened his expression, intensely aware of how many people depended on him getting this right.

Miranda saw something in Theo's eyes—a tiny flame. Fanned into life by love? Had they both been struck by the same thunderbolt?

The thought filled her with happiness. 'If you put it like that, then my answer has to be…yes.'

'Yes?' Catching hold of her hands, Theo raised them passionately to his lips. 'You have just made me the happiest man in the world, Miranda.'

CHAPTER SIX

'MIRANDA has agreed to marry me.'

Six words that had changed her life the moment they were spoken; six words that travelled around Kalmos like wildfire and were in the public domain almost immediately after that.

Miranda watched horrorstruck as the news broke on satellite TV. She should have known. She should have thought things through and understood the implications. But here she was in Agalia's snug home, on a remote Greek island, with a mobile phone that refused to work and a landline that was for ever engaged. Her parents, her twin sister Emily—everyone she cared about back home—were about to hear the news that she should have told them face to face. And if they hadn't picked it up on television they would hardly miss the announcement in the papers the next day. If the television anchorman's excitement was anything to go by, the news would make headlines across the world. It wasn't every day that the Greek billionaire heir to a shipping dynasty chose a bride. The fact that Theo Savakis was to marry the musician Miranda Weston had only added fuel to an already raging fire—and she could only sit there raging with frustration.

She had moved into the taverna as Theo had asked, to keep her safe from the paparazzi until their wedding. She hadn't given a thought to legitimate news hounds, let alone the paparazzi! She hated matters moving so swiftly out of her control. What had seemed the only right thing to do was already beginning to feel like a monumental mistake, and she couldn't bear to think that she might have made a second serious error of judgement. The last time she had placed her trust in a man there had been terrible consequences.

The phone calls to her family were the hardest she had ever had to make. They had always been close, but hearing her father's throat tighten when he spoke told her that he thought she had become a stranger whose behaviour he could no longer predict. Her mother had enthused, and had hardly seemed to care that a neighbour had told her first. The only thing that mattered, she said, was that Miranda was safely and splendidly 'set up in life'.

She couldn't blame her mother for enjoying the moment. From humble beginnings, on a modest housing estate, one daughter had won the heart of a prince while the other was on her way to marrying a Greek tycoon. But still Miranda yearned for her father's down-to-earth take on life. His common sense and inward satisfaction with even her smallest achievement was worth more than all the fanfares in the world. He had never asked her to be a world-class musician, he had only wanted her to make a difference. Would she be able to do that when the doors of the Savakis citadel had closed behind her?

She could picture her father trying to calm her mother's triumphant glee as he pointed out that their daughter would be facing the same pressures as any bride, and that marriage to a man like Theo Savakis would be fraught with its own problems. Having delivered such a momentous piece of news, she could hardly ring them back and say she'd changed her mind. And, on the positive side, at least her mother had something to focus on, so that when she discovered the truth about the repercussions from the accident it wouldn't come as such a blow.

The call to her twin sister Emily left her feeling particularly low, because she sensed it had made the rift between them deeper. Emily was still hurt from the way Miranda had pushed her away after the accident, and all she said was, 'But why, Miranda?' She must have repeated that phrase a dozen times. They had never kept things from each other before the accident. What would have been the point when each of them knew what the other was thinking?

The difference between her own family and Theo's was marked. The little she knew of his background sounded so sterile she doubted he had ever experienced emotion until the business world had claimed him. She could understand the attraction. Business gave him something tangible to grab hold of, balance sheets, reports, his own huge and sustained success; all of those cogs in a very visible wheel. Love was different. Love defied analysis. And its path could not be predicted in a neatly bound five-year plan.

So why had she got herself into this situation? Why had she agreed to marry Theo Savakis, a man she hardly knew? Was love enough?

Except, considering it, Miranda realised that life without Theo was already unthinkable. So that was her answer.

'Theo!' Her face lit up as he walked into the room. 'I've finished my calls.'

'Was everyone all right with our news?'

'Well, it came a bit of a shock.'

'That's only to be expected,' he pointed out.

'My mother took it well.'

'That must reassure you.'

No, Miranda realised, it hadn't. Her father was a tender, trusting soul, and she had bulldozed his concerns with a false bravado he had picked up on right away. And she still felt bad about Emily.

'Well, Agalia's excited too.' Theo placed his hands lightly on her shoulders as he spoke. 'Spiros tells me that she's already planning the wedding…'

'The wedding?' Since the accident she had often sought escape in a dream world where everything was lovely and nothing difficult or bad or dramatic ever happened. She had to snap out of it. This wedding was going to happen.

'You look surprised.' Theo frowned. 'There's no reason for delay, is there?'

'Well… Obviously I'd like my family to attend…'

His face relaxed. 'Is that all? I'll bring them over in the jet.'

Miranda felt panicked for a moment. This was a world she didn't understand, a world where anything was possible—for Theo. 'Of course. I hadn't thought of that.'

'Don't worry, it's going to be wonderful.' Coming to kneel at her feet, he took her hands and kissed her damaged fingers one by one. 'And we're going to sort this out too…'

She gritted her teeth. He meant so well, but she just wanted the moment to be over.

'And this isn't the only part of you I want to heal,' he added, seeing her expression. 'There's here, too.' Lightly touching her chest above her heart, he smiled reassuringly.

Miranda smiled back. She felt she should.

Weddings in Greece required a certain amount of red tape, but for men like Theo Savakis, Miranda soon discovered, the rules everyone else was obliged to follow did not apply.

She was racing pell-mell into the unknown, she realised anxiously as they discussed possible dates for their wedding over dinner that night at the taverna.

'I don't want to rush you,' he'd said.

But he did, she sensed, wondering why. Remembering Agalia's excitement, she put her doubts aside. 'Agalia has arranged for my wedding dress to be made here on the island—'

'Here on Kalmos? But I was going to take you to Paris.'

'You don't have to take me to Paris, Theo.' She touched his hand to console him, because he looked so disappointed. 'I couldn't possibly let Agalia down by insisting on some other dressmaker.' She could see Theo was battling to control the impulse to disagree with her. He was accustomed to having everything his own way, but that would have to change. She had no intention of spending her married life following orders.

'All right,' he agreed eventually. 'If you're sure that's what you want. I suppose a simple wedding dress will be more appropriate for such a low-key wedding—'

It was a strange use of words. What was he saying? Suddenly the paranoia from her former life and the suspicions she'd had about Theo flooded back. 'Why? Do you mean it will look good, Theo? Show you in a better light to the rest of the world? The Greek tycoon who appreciates the simple things in life and so marries a damaged woman in order to prove it?'

'What?' He stared at her, aghast. 'Is that what you think of me?'

'I don't know, Theo. I don't know what to think! Why are you marrying me in such a rush?'

'You know why! Because I love you, and some things can't wait.'

Something still bothered her, but she had nothing to go on. Why was a man like Theo Savakis getting married to someone he hardly knew on a tiny island in the middle of nowhere in such a rush? And why was she going along with it so complacently? Was it because this was the easiest way out for her? Was this a head-in-the-sand escape to a handsome, wealthy man who could provide her with all the distraction she needed to forget the nightmares, to forget what had happened to her arm?

'I don't give a damn what our marriage looks like in the eyes of the world,' he insisted, reclaiming her attention. 'The only people who matter are you and me, and after that all the people we care about. I'm surprised it even crossed your mind to doubt my motives. Don't you know me at all?'

'No, Theo, that's the trouble. I really don't.'

Instead of retaliating, as she had expected, he went quite still—as if he had his own doubts to subdue. But then gradually she saw all the old confidence and humour returning to his face.

'Are we having our first argument?' He slanted her a grin.

How could she remain angry with Theo when he looked at her like that? She was suffering from a bad case of pre-wedding nerves, and that was all. She took a deep, steadying breath and told him as much.

'Are you worried about the wedding night?' He had meant it as a joke, and was surprised to see all the blood drain from her face. She looked so young sometimes, so vulnerable...

'No, of course not.'

Her denial sounded hollow, and that worried him. In fact he'd been worried ever since she had made her phone calls home. She had become like a tyre running flat; all the pep had gone out of her. He could understand her family's concern. They knew what it was like for her to be in the public eye— they had lived through it once before.

'I understand your unease after speaking to your family, Miranda,' he assured her. 'They know what you're taking on. But remember I'll be at your side every step of the way. I won't let anything or anyone harm you. And as for our wedding night—' *Theos*, her eyes were wide and troubled; she made him feel like Bluebeard. Reaching across the table, he took her hand. 'I love you. What more can I say?'

Desire might be eating away at him, but he could and he would control it. He had a lot to gain from the marriage, and he wanted to make sure it was successful. He wanted Miranda to be happy, and awakening her to the pleasures of the marriage bed was just one way he could ensure that she was.

'Have I reassured you?' He held her gaze until *he* was reassured, and then turned to lighter things to distract her. 'So, the wedding dress and honeymoon are taken care of...' He ticked them off on his fingers.

'Honeymoon?'

'At least we won't have to travel far...'

'Of course—we're already here,' she guessed, and this time the smile slowly made its way up to her eyes.

She was like a child who wanted to be happy again but who didn't dare believe that she could be, he realised. It made him want to make everything perfect for her. 'There's nowhere on earth more beautiful than Kalmos.' He hoped his eyes reflected all the love he felt for his island, and for Miranda, and that it would shore up her fragile faith in him. 'I hope you're not too disappointed?'

'Disappointed? No, of course I'm not disappointed. Kalmos is the perfect place for a honeymoon...and an idyllic setting for a wedding.'

Her declaration prompted him to say, 'I know we're still building trust in each other, Miranda, and I can see how you must think it strange for me to want to get married with so little fuss. But the truth is Kalmos is my favourite place on earth, and I want to share it with you.'

'What are you doing?' she asked as he dug into the pocket of his shirt.

He had been longing to give her something, and now seeing her face wary but excited was everything he'd hoped for. 'This is for you.' He held it out to her. 'Would you like to try it on and see if it fits?'

'This can't be for me!'

She sounded amazed, and it touched him. She stared spell-bound as he eased the wide gold band studded with diamonds onto her wedding finger.

'You don't need to give me a gift like this. It must be very valuable.'

'I want to give it to you. It's a family heirloom. Don't you like it?'

'Of course I do. It's fabulous.' Even as she admired the jewels, Miranda shrank a little inside. She felt as if Theo's high expectations of a wife were encapsulated in his gift of the priceless ring.

'The stones are flawless,' he pointed out.

For a flawed bride? Her disability had never weighed more heavily than it did in that moment. But then Theo drew her to her feet and, raising her hands to his lips, kissed each of her fingers very gently. The intensity of feeling she felt for him was frightening. Theo Savakis could have any woman in the world. He was always so tender with her...but what if he woke up one morning and saw her as damaged goods?

The next day Theo persuaded Miranda to come out on his yacht. He had business to do, he said, and couldn't bear for them to be apart. Agalia was resigned to the plan because Theo's yacht was like a bustling city; the chance of them being alone on a working day was remote.

During the morning Miranda was alarmed to overhear snatches of Theo's conversation while he was talking on the satellite phone. He had left her side and walked a few steps away to ensure his privacy, but one of the less admirable traits of being a musician was the enhanced hearing that allowed her to eavesdrop. An elderly aunt had once accused her of having 'ears on stalks', because she possessed more than the ability to distinguish fine differences in pitch and volume— she could also detect the softest note, the faintest sound.

What she heard was Theo discussing the date of their wedding. 'It can be changed if necessary,' he snapped.

Who was he talking to? And why would he change the date of their wedding without talking to her first? Was this how life was going to be from now on? Ordered at Theo's whim? Blind obedience had never been part of their agreement!

The moment he finished the call she asked him if something was wrong. Before Theo had a chance to answer a member of crew approached with another message for him. She had expected him to be busy, and had brought books to amuse herself, but she sensed that something out of the ordinary was unfolding. Because of it, she curbed her impatience and waited to see what he would say.

Eventually he slipped back into the seat at her side. 'I've been neglecting you. I apologise.'

She waited. She could hardly challenge him and admit to being an eavesdropper. 'Don't worry, I've got everything I need.'

As Theo hummed distractedly she gathered his mind was on anything other than whether she had a cool drink to hand, or enough sun lotion.

So what was happening? She had learned that Kalmos was the island of his birth, and he had talked of moving back into his ancestral home on the far side of the island. She had no idea who lived there now, or what the house might be like; Theo was sparing with adjectives, and 'big' told her nothing. Maybe a problem connected with the property had occurred? Perhaps it wouldn't be ready to move in to by the time they were married and the wedding might have to be postponed?

A prescient shiver coursed down Miranda's spine, telling her it wasn't that.

'Are you cold?'

'No... I was worried when I saw your face, that's all. The phone call?' she prompted.

'It was business.' He shrugged dismissively.

'Business?' She saw a muscle working in his jaw. 'Well, as long as it's nothing that can interfere with our wedding...'

'What makes you say that?'

She shook her head. 'An over-active imagination, I hope.'

Leaning towards her, he took her hand. 'I promise it was just a business call. Nothing is going to get in the way of our wedding.'

'Not even business, Theo?' She said it lightly, but she sensed that he didn't appreciate the interrogation.

'What do I have to say to convince you?'

'Tell me that you love me,' she said honestly, laying her soul bare for him. 'Tell me that you won't let anything come between us...'

He smiled. 'That's far too easy.'

As his lips tugged up and the warmth flooded back into his eyes she had to believe him.

Holding her gaze, Theo took her hand and kissed it gently. 'And as for loving you...I can't believe you still need my reassurance. Of course I love you, Miranda. I've promised to look after you for the rest of your life, haven't I?'

A hollow opened up inside her at his words. Was that it? She felt like a worthy cause he had taken under his wing.

Theo hated lying to her. He had never lied to anyone in his life before. He had never needed to. And now, even though it wasn't strictly a lie, he was deceiving her. The call *had* been about business—about everything he had devoted his adult life to building up. And in a way he had told her the truth too: the wedding wouldn't be spoiled or cancelled. If anything, it would be brought forward. He would have to wait for the doctor's report before he could make a final decision.

He had been warned that the old guard were hovering like vultures round a wounded beast. When Dimitri died it was imperative that the Savakis shipping line remained under his control, and if that meant marrying Miranda rather sooner than either of them had anticipated, then that was what he would do. He could not sacrifice the livelihoods of thousands of families for the sake of decorum and a few hours' delay. If Dimitri's illness was as serious as rumour said, they would marry at once.

'No, Theo! Absolutely not!'

Miranda couldn't even pretend to hide her shock.

Closing the door of the small office at the taverna to give them some privacy, Theo leaned back against it. 'I know this must have come as a surprise to you, and so I'm giving you time to think about it before you give me your final answer—'

'How long, Theo? Five minutes?'

He tipped his head, suggesting *maybe*, and said nothing.

'And if I disagree with your request to bring our marriage forward?'

He remained silent, telling her everything she needed to know.

'Marrying tomorrow is out of the question. I don't know how you can even ask me to do that. What's got into you? Have you forgotten my family? What about the wonderful day we had planned? Or are we just going to rush through our wedding as if you are ashamed of me, as if pledging our lives to each other counts for nothing?'

'Ashamed of you?' The words leapt out at him. How could she possibly think that? But then, seeing her unconsciously nursing her arm, he understood.

Leaning over the desk, he planted his fists so he could stare straight into her eyes. 'You're beautiful, Miranda. Every part of you is beautiful. And I'm proud that you have agreed to be my bride. It's more than I deserve.'

And now he was ashamed of himself. Seeing tears well up in Miranda's eyes told him she was reassured, but saying she was more than he deserved was too close to the truth. He had so much to gain from this marriage, and for the first time since all the pieces of the jigsaw had fallen so logically into place he found himself staring at the picture he had made and hating what he saw.

'Will you hear me out?' he asked her gently. He was confident he had left nothing to chance. The wedding would go ahead the next day—it had to. The latest bulletin said Dimitri was failing fast but had rallied sufficiently to demand proof that their contract would be honoured. Success or failure rested on Miranda. Theo must gain her agreement to the hasty wedding, but above all he wanted her to do so willingly.

'Don't worry about your family.' Going round the desk, he took hold of her hands. 'I have a plan.' Cupping her chin, he made her look at him. 'Don't ask me to wait, Miranda…' And when she started to protest he silenced her with a kiss.

'Okay,' she said reluctantly. 'What's your plan?'

Her eyes were wounded and she was still suspicious. He had to look away when she searched his eyes. 'We will have the civil ceremony tomorrow, and then a few days later we will have a public celebration—a blessing on our marriage with all your family present—'

'A blessing here on the island?'

'Yes. I'll fly everyone over.' It was a nice touch, and he was pleased that he had thought of it. 'I think your family would like that.' He waited tensely to see what she would say.

'We'd have to make sure the date was convenient for everyone.'

Relief flooded over him. 'Of course. I'm sure we'll find a suitable date—and don't worry about the ceremony tomorrow. It won't go unmarked. Agalia has already started the preparations—'

Her mouth fell open. 'You told Agalia before you told me?'

He had to harden his heart and take whatever she threw at him. 'Only so she could start getting everything ready...' But his excuse fell on stony ground.

'This is a *fait accompli*, isn't it, Theo? I have no say in it at all!'

Everyone thought business was hard at his level, but they were wrong. *This* was hard. 'You know how much I want you, Miranda. Don't make this difficult for me...' Instead of softening, her gaze hardened, and she pulled back when he tried to embrace her.

'I don't understand why we must change our plans and bring the wedding forward—and why go to the trouble of a second ceremony? Why not wait for my family to arrive, as we agreed, and have all the celebrations on the same day?' Getting to her feet, she went to stare out of the window with her back turned to him.

'Why all the questions, Miranda? It seems perfectly obvious to me.'

She turned. 'Then perhaps you'd care to explain your reasoning?'

That he couldn't do. 'I can't believe you aren't excited.' He was growing impatient, and in fact he felt quite wounded. Surely any bride should be delighted at the prospect of an eager husband? And his commitments to the business wouldn't wait.

She looked startled at his tone, then visibly made an effort to speak calmly. 'So your suggestion is that we marry tomorrow, quietly, with just a couple of witnesses?'

'Agalia and Spiros. Perfect, yes?' He was smiling, relieved that she had seen the sense of it. Dimitri might be a warhorse, but even Dimitri couldn't hold back the tide of mortality. It was crucial that he moved fast.

Miranda shook her head. 'There's more to this than you're telling me, Theo.'

'Are you calling me a liar?'

She didn't speak for a moment, letting him draw his own conclusions, and then she said, 'You tell me that you love me, and that you want to court me properly and respectfully, in the old-fashioned way—'

'I do!' He bit back the other things he wanted to say to defend his position. He did love her—if love meant wanting a woman in your bed, wanting her and no other to bear your children, wanting her soothing and reliable presence waiting for you when you'd had a stressful day's work...

'And yet a man in your position wants to rush everything through on this tiny remote island?'

'I love you, and I want you with me always, Miranda. *Theos!* I've given you my reasons—'

And then the penny dropped. Of course. Miranda's twin had married a prince at the cathedral in Ferara. He took a moment to calm down.

'I'm not trying to rush things through or hide you away. I'm sure that if you asked your brother-in-law Alessandro whether he would have preferred to take Emily away and marry her quietly rather than share such a precious moment with hordes of strangers, you would find Alessandro would envy us...' He saw with relief that at last he had said something she could agree with.

Miranda couldn't work him out. Did she know Theo at all?

Or was she back in that half-world where reality could conveniently be put on hold? Kalmos was supposed to have been the setting for her climb back, her fight back—but how far was she going to get when she couldn't even trust the man she loved?

And why was she feeling so heated, so uncertain? Theo's promise of a formal blessing on their marriage with all her family present was such a romantic idea. And a village wedding too—what could be lovelier?

And he was right. Hadn't Emily been almost unbearably tense on her wedding day, fully aware that the eyes of the world were on her? Theo was sparing her all that, and she was shouting at him.

'I'm sorry, Theo. I'm overreacting... I must be suffering from pre-wedding nerves.'

He softened immediately. 'You don't have to apologise, Miranda. It's my fault for being so impatient.' Taking her hands, he raised them to his lips and kissed them reverently. 'Do you agree to my plan?'

They would be the centre of media attention soon enough. One day of privacy in which to make their solemn vows was the most precious gift Theo could have given her. 'I agree,' she said softly.

'You've made the right decision,' he assured her, and she felt the tension in him relax.

'It's wonderful!' Agalia exclaimed when Miranda told her the news after lunch. 'It's so romantic! I knew the moment Theo told me he wanted to marry you that it would have to be soon. And now he is bringing the wedding forward! Don't worry— it's no trouble to me. The dress can be finished quickly, the feast prepared in an instant, and Spiros already has a new waistcoat...'

How could she give voice to all her worries about the future in the face of such enthusiasm? Miranda forced her concerns back behind a smile. As far as Agalia and Spiros were concerned Theo was the most wonderful man on earth. She was on her own when it came to doubting his motives for bringing the wedding forward.

'Tomorrow! Just think of it!' Agalia enthused, breaking into her thoughts.

'Tomorrow…' Miranda heard a faint note of alarm in her own voice.

'Don't tell me you had forgotten the day of our wedding, Miranda?'

'Theo!' Miranda turned and smiled at him. 'I didn't see you there.'

'You're a very lucky man, Theo!' Agalia embraced him.

'You think I don't know that?' As he gently disentangled himself Theo saw that at the sight of him Miranda's face might have been lit from the inside. For all her concerns about the hasty wedding she was resilient and adaptable; she was a woman he would be proud to call his wife. He produced the bouquet of flowers he was holding behind his back with a flourish.

'You spoil me,' she said, smiling up at him.

'I haven't even started to do that yet,' he murmured, holding her gaze.

'I'll leave you two alone,' Agalia said happily. 'But I'll be just inside my room, Theo, and I think I'd better keep my door open.'

'Quite right,' he agreed. 'You can't be too careful when there are ardent suitors on the premises.'

'You think I don't know that?' She slapped his arm playfully on her way past.

'I thought you would be too busy to come and see me this afternoon, Theo.' She looked up—but Miranda never just looked at him: she plumbed his soul. 'What's wrong?' she asked.

He tensed. She could read him like a book. Some of his advisors thought it would be better for the wedding to be held immediately—in the dark, if necessary! He had disagreed. There were only so many times he could manipulate the woman he intended to marry. 'Nothing's wrong,' he said evenly, 'other than my impatience to hold you in my arms.'

'Well, you'd better control yourself with Agalia outside the door.'

Miranda's humour was back, and with it her confidence. He thanked God for it. But how long would he be able to keep the truth about their marriage a secret? For ever, he hoped. But Miranda was bright and quick, and if she ever found out the real reason behind the hastily arranged ceremony she would be devastated...

It was too late to think like that, too late to turn back the clock. He was committed to a path and nothing could stop the wheels of fate turning.

CHAPTER SEVEN

MIRANDA'S throat was so tight she could hardly answer Agalia's questions. It was early morning, and she was dressing for her wedding. Sunlight was streaming in through the windows of her bedroom at the taverna, lighting the rugs hanging on the whitewashed walls.

The colourful hangings provided the perfect backdrop for her gown—a dress so beautiful she defied any of the top fashion houses in Paris to produce anything lovelier. Layer upon layer of silk chiffon billowed at her slightest movement, and the dress was cunningly cut so that when she stood perfectly still it clung to her like a sheath. The dressmaker had interpreted her wishes faultlessly: nothing fancy, no long and cumbersome trains, and no ornate trimmings. It was a dream of a dress, with a pure and simple line.

It was only the colour over which she was agonising now.

Right from the start Theo had tried to put her at her ease, joking that if a man waited for a virgin he would wait for ever. He thought her concerns about their wedding night were all wrapped up in whether she was a virgin or not, and had insisted that the past was the past, and all he cared about was their future together.

He made it all sound so simple, but it wasn't simple. She

wasn't a virgin, but she wasn't experienced either. And though her body wanted Theo, her memories told her that she hated sex. And the dress was snowy white, which she found both symbolic and alarming.

She wished she knew more, and could be more confident about the role Theo would expect her to play in the bedroom. She felt such a fool, knowing that she had forged a career, was even reasonably attractive, and yet was so ignorant about sex—something everyone else seemed to take for granted...

Agalia had finished lacing the gown. '*Kalo!* Good. We are ready,' she declared with satisfaction.

'Thank you.' Miranda's voice wobbled.

'Tears, Miranda? But this should be the happiest day of your life.'

And maybe it might have been, if she hadn't been beset by doubts. She could never be the sophisticated lover a man like Theo deserved. He was highly charged, sexually in the prime of his life. He would expect an explosion of passion on their wedding night, and all he was likely to get was a damp squib. And his moods worried her too. Try as he might, Theo could not hide the fact that something was on his mind. Was he having second thoughts?

'I know,' Agalia said, clapping her hands and reclaiming Miranda's attention. 'They are tears of happiness.'

'That's right, Agalia,' Miranda agreed, grateful for the let-out. 'Can I hear music?' She seized eagerly on the distraction. 'Is that the wedding party?'

Unlike her charge, Agalia was beside herself with excitement as she ran to the window. 'Yes, they're here! They're here!'

Joining Agalia at the window, even Miranda smiled as she leaned out and waved to the boisterous villagers streaming down the beach. It looked as if everyone in the village had turned out for her wedding. Far from it being a hole-and-corner affair, as she had feared, the whole population of Kalmos seemed to be on the march. Her spirits lifted. Sharing the day with all the people who had made her so welcome would make it special for her.

Two elderly musicians were leading the procession, one of them playing a fiddle and the other an ancient instrument Miranda recognised as an aoud. She frowned as they continued on past the taverna. 'Are they going without me?'

'No, of course not,' Agalia reassured her. 'They are on their way to collect Theo from his yacht in the harbour, and when they have done that they will come back here for you.'

'How long will that take?'

Agalia laughed. 'You make it sound as if you are dreading Theo's arrival!'

Agalia had no idea how close to the truth she had come, Miranda realised as she dipped her head and allowed the Greek woman to place a simple headdress of fresh flowers on her hair. She was going into this marriage blindfold, and dragging decent people like Agalia and Spiros along with her. 'I'm not dreading his arrival...'

'Then what?' Agalia pressed gently.

'I'm concerned that we have only known each other a short time.'

'Now, you listen to me.' Agalia spoke sternly as she drew Miranda round to face her. 'Theo is a good man, Miranda. I've known him all his life, and you are the woman for him. Do you think Theo is such a fool that he has made the decision to marry you lightly? Or that he would bring the wedding forward unless he had a very good reason for doing so? And I think we both know what that reason is...' Her eyes began to twinkle, but then she turned serious again. 'Theo rescued the Savakis shipping line and turned it into a world-class company. Do you think that was by chance? No. Theo wouldn't be marrying you unless he had the very best reason for doing so. And his reason is that he loves you, Miranda.'

'I hope you're right.'

'Of course I'm right. I'm standing in the place of your mother today, and if she were here she would say what I am saying—that all brides are nervous on their wedding day. But you have no need to worry because you are marrying a wonderful man who will take care of you and cherish you for the rest of your life.'

Miranda couldn't bear for Agalia to see all the doubt in her eyes. She turned away. 'Is is time to put on my veil?'

'Yes, it's time. Sandals?' Agalia reminded her when the veil was fixed, taking them out of the protective tissue paper and placing them on the floor for Miranda to step into.

As she slipped her feet into the dainty beaded mules Miranda caught sight of her reflection in the mirror. Agalia had polished her hair with silk, so that it shone blue-black in the light, and she was wearing it down so that it fell almost to her waist. With the white dress and the crown of flowers the transformation was marked. She looked so young—serene and docile, like a sacrifice.

'Miranda, come. We must hurry.'

Miranda started as Agalia's voice called her back from her trance. She had to snap out of it. She was being melodramatic—and if you looked hard enough for trouble you would always find some.

'I can hear them!' Agalia exclaimed.

Raising her chin, Miranda went up to Agalia and embraced her. 'Thank you for everything you've done for me. I'm going to have a wonderful wedding day thanks to you.'

'These are for you, Miranda.'

She was shaking, Miranda realised. She had to take a long,

steadying breath before she could lift her head and smile into Theo's eyes.

'Take the flowers,' he prompted.

Everyone was silent as they waited for her to do so.

'Theo...' His name rang between them. There was such intensity in his gaze, and Miranda was thankful for the gossamer veil masking her own turbulent emotions.

'Are you ready?' He smiled encouragement.

People were jostling for position in an effort to see her. Everyone was dressed casually, in a way that perfectly suited the sunny climate and picturesque setting. Even Theo was wearing traditional clothes rather than a formal wedding suit. Miranda was surprised, but thought the white linen shirt he wore loose over trousers made from the same fabric reinforced his raw masculinity. The black waistcoat, heavily embroidered with gold, complemented his fierce glamour, and his strong, tanned feet in the simple thonged sandals gave her such a sexual charge she had to look away.

'Miranda?'

Theo was growing impatient, and soon the crowd would be too. She waved as she stepped forward, and was touched when everyone cheered. The wave of enthusiasm bolstered her up as she walked into the brilliant sunlight and took her place at Theo's side.

The simple wedding ceremony touched Miranda deeply. And she could hardly wait to share her happiness with their wedding guests. But at the taverna she discovered that Theo's business had no respect for a bride on her wedding day. He had already been called away to take a phone call.

She took her place without him at the top table, and for a while chatted animatedly with the guests on either side. But as time went on she grew increasingly disappointed, and eventually angry. Surely Theo could put his wedding before his business commitments? After all, it was only one day.

She could see him still talking rapidly inside the taverna, receiver clenched tightly in his hand. It had to be a crisis or he would have explained that the call was interrupting his wedding feast. She must be patient, and ready to support him if there was trouble. Hadn't she felt that same level of commitment in her own career?

But the light was fading and people were hungry. Gathering round the barbecue, they were casting surreptitious glances at the top table—specifically at the empty place at her side. And Agalia had gone to so much trouble—it would be dreadful if the food began to spoil...

Miranda's attention was drawn to the heavy gold wedding band she was unconsciously twirling around her finger. Unmistakably Hellenic in design, it was intricately etched and studded with diamonds. When she had commented on its age and beauty, Theo had asked her what she expected when she was marrying into a family who could trace their origins back to Mount Olympus. At the time they had both laughed, but right now she didn't find it so funny. Was this what it meant to be married into a family like Theo's? Did he think she could be put on hold whenever it suited him, like some latter-day Penelope? If there was a crisis, why didn't he share it with her? If there was no crisis, why couldn't he ask the caller to ring back after their wedding feast?

Guests had started expressing their concern more openly, and there was a distinct rumble of unease as they stared at her. She couldn't just sit in her place as if nothing was wrong. Rising from her seat, she lifted up her skirts and made her apologies.

She found Theo still talking on the telephone. 'Theo—'

He put up his hand to silence her. 'I'll only be a few minutes. Would you mind waiting for me outside?'

His tone astounded her. She was his wife now—not some minion to be ordered out of the room. 'Yes, I would mind.' Miranda kept her voice low and closed the door carefully behind her. 'Our guests are waiting. We can't just abandon them.'

He gave her a savage look, but then, quite suddenly, and to her relief, the cloud hanging over him seemed to lift.

'You're right, and I apologise,' he said, covering the mouthpiece. 'This call has taken a lot longer than I anticipated. Please forgive me, *thespinis mou*, I will be with you in a moment.'

'I'll wait here until you finish.'

With a brief nod he turned away, and fired off a few more words in Greek before cutting the line.

'Was it so important?' Miranda reined in her anger, seeing the tension lines on Theo's face. 'Do you have a problem? Can I help you with anything?'

Coming up to her, Theo traced the line of her face with his finger. 'You are so gentle and so good, and you have already helped me just by being here.'

'Can't you tell me?'

Theo silenced her question with a kiss.

'Should I be worried?' she said, when he let her go.

Capturing a strand of her silky hair, he wound it around his finger. 'No, *pethi mou*, there's nothing for you to worry about. It was only a business call, Miranda. I hope you know that I wouldn't leave you alone for a moment unless I had to—'

'*Had* to? And yet you dismiss the call as *only* business?'

He dropped the coil of hair and pulled away. 'Don't quiz me, Miranda.'

'Then please don't behave so badly towards our guests!'

'Agalia and Spiros are taking care of everyone for us…'

Following his glance, she saw Theo was right. 'That still doesn't excuse our absence, Theo.'

She recoiled as he snapped, 'You should remember that you're my wife now! You must learn to fit in.'

'To whatever small space you can find for me in your diary? I don't think so, Theo. I think you should remember that right now our marriage is nothing more than a piece of paper, and I can still walk away from it!'

Briefly, he looked stunned, and then, catching hold of her upper arms, he brought her back to him. 'I've never seen you in a temper before, Miranda…and I think I like it.'

As Theo stared down into her face his lips drew her gaze. She fought him off for a second, but he was too strong for her, and when he deepened the kiss she responded hungrily.

'Damn this wedding feast,' he husked fiercely against her neck when he let her go. 'Damn all interruptions! If you want me to make this marriage something more than a piece of paper I'm happy to oblige right now—'

'Then why wait?'

Silence hung between them as they both took in what she had said. Theo couldn't have been more surprised by her blatant suggestion, Miranda realised. But here in the shadows she felt little would be expected of her and maybe it would be all right. It was the set-piece drama of her wedding night on Theo's yacht that she was dreading.

'Are you asking me to kiss you again?' His voice hinted that he was open to suggestions.

'Yes, I'd like that…to begin with.' She met his gaze steadily.

'But not here?' He frowned.

His wife was a mass of contradictions. Inexperienced, even nervous, but then suddenly she was easing her shoulders back to reveal the deep valley between her breasts, making his senses roar.

'We can't stay here.' Even as he said the words he could

feel the tightening in his groin. Miranda's eagerness for intimacy was a revelation to him. 'Have you forgotten our guests?'

'They're busy eating now, and soon they will be dancing…'

Glancing out of the window, he saw she was right. No one would care if they were absent for a little while longer. He pulled the blind.

A single ray of light still managed to escape. It was enough for him to see everything she was offering him beneath the filmy chiffon of her gown: the curve of her thighs, the rosy swell of engorged nipples, the provocative line of her belly. He wanted nothing more than to pleasure her, to savour her responses…

Cupping her face tenderly in his hands, he brushed her lips with his mouth and drank in her sigh. She was pliant and relaxed, her limbs like liquid gold, and she was his. It was like drinking at the deepest well of the coolest water in the hottest part of the day…

But was this what he wanted? Was he going to make love to his bride for the first time in the back room of a taverna?

'No, Miranda. This isn't right.' Very gently he unlocked her hands from behind his neck and brought them to his lips to kiss them in turn.

'Don't you want me?'

He smiled against her mouth as he whispered, 'Of course I want you. But when I make love to you for the first time I want it to be something we remember for ever…'

'So why can't it be here?'

'Because there are better places to make love than on a table in a taverna. If you have a little patience, I will show you.'

Maybe some women would have been happy as they waited for a night of passion with their lover, but for Miranda it was the most refined torture Theo could have devised for her.

'And now it really is time to join our wedding guests,' Theo said, dropping a kiss on her brow.

But he still hadn't given her an explanation for his lengthy call, Miranda realised as he slipped his arm around her waist and steered her towards the door.

CHAPTER EIGHT

THE wedding party came to an end when Miranda was least expecting it. Theo swept her into his arms in the middle of a dance. Weaving his way across the crowded dance floor, he carried her down the steps of the taverna and onto the beach. The two musicians who had led the procession earlier spotted them and, seizing their instruments, drew the wedding guests after them like Pied Pipers.

Theo strode on, with everyone singing and dancing in his wake. The moon was like a beacon in the sky, and the sky was a star-studded canopy over their heads. But the vigour had gone out of their guests, Miranda noticed when she glanced behind. Or maybe Theo was simply outpacing everyone. Certainly his vigour was undiminished.

The distance between the taverna and the harbour melted away quickly, and soon the monstrous shadow of Theo's yacht loomed ahead of them. She could feel her heart thundering, and was sure Theo must feel it too. This was everything she had hoped for—the beginning of her new life with the man she loved. But she was frightened she was going to lose him on their first night together as man and wife. And, much as she hated herself for still doubting him, it wasn't just the sex she was dreading. She couldn't rid herself of the feeling that nothing was ever as good as it seemed. And this was so good…

Striding up the gangplank, Theo drew to a halt and lowered her gently to the deck as if she was precious porcelain. Or his best investment yet.

Miranda brushed the rogue thought aside. Her imagination was running away with her.

The remaining guests had caught up with them. Putting his arm around her waist, Theo drew her close. Everyone was clustered around the foot of the gangplank, waving, and when Miranda waved back they all cheered.

At this cue, Theo took a velvet pouch from one of his crew and handed it to her.

'What do I do with this?' She smiled, forgetting her doubts. They seemed ridiculous now.

'It's another of our traditions,' Theo said, 'and one I think you'll like.'

Peering inside the pouch, Miranda saw that it was full of sugared almonds. 'To eat?'

He laughed, 'Not unless you want a riot. Throw them—like this…' He showered the waiting crowd, and then took charge of a second pouch as everyone applauded.

'But you've got gold coins!'

'So that everyone can share in our good fortune.'

Miranda felt another frisson of superstitious alarm, but, remembering her vow to keep her imagination in check, quickly followed Theo's lead.

When the pouches were empty, and everyone had drifted away after calling their good wishes, Theo escorted her onto the aft deck.

'You think of everything.' Miranda gazed around, hardly able to believe that all this had been prepared for their pleasure.

'I have an excellent crew.' Drawing her arm through his,

Theo brought her to an alcove where an unbleached linen canopy had been erected to protect them from the breeze. So many candles had been lit that even the night was held at bay, and a small group of musicians was playing to one side of a buffet table.

They sat at an intimate table laid for two, then danced to the sinuous rhythms of South America beneath a sky thick with stars. As the pulse of the music thrummed Miranda felt all her worries melting away. She was safe in Theo's arms, safe and confident. She had been wrong to look for trouble, wrong to be so angry when he had wanted to bring the wedding forward. Instead of challenging Theo she should be rejoicing because she had found a man who loved her so much.

As if sensing the turn her thoughts were taking, he dropped a chaste kiss on her brow. But its very innocence was provocative, particularly when the touch of his hands held so much promise. She wondered if Theo knew the effect he was having on her with just the smallest adjustment of his grip. Relaxing into him, she dared the doubts to assail her now.

'Are you hungry?' he murmured.

The expression in his eyes made a quiver of arousal run right through her. 'I'm starving…'

'Then shall we?'

Miranda wasn't surprised when Theo led her straight past the buffet table and on towards the companionway that led to his sumptuous quarters on board the yacht. And by the time he carried her over the threshold of his stateroom she was shivering with anticipation rather than fear.

The room had been subtly lit, and was lightly fragranced with sandalwood. There was a deep fur rug on the polished wooden floor, and the sheets on the huge circular bed were black satin. It was like a set from a film, Miranda mused dreamily as Theo softly closed the door behind them.

Leaning back against it, he stared down at her. 'Welcome to my world, Miranda.'

There was such a mix of emotion on his face. Tenderness, desire, and even something close to triumph. She felt it like a cloud briefly covering the sun, and realised that she would have to remind him that she would always be her own person: two in one, not one and a bit. But there was all the time in the world for that...

And when he kissed her his lips were so cherishing, so loving, she forgot. It was as if Theo, recognising her inexperience, wanted to reassure her, and in the end it was she who showed him what she wanted with the touch of her hands and the press of her body.

Drawing back, he studied her face in silence for a moment, and then kissed her again, deeply, in a way that touched her soul. His palms were warm and firm as they moved down her arms, but even then she wasn't prepared for him taking hold of her damaged hand and raising it so he could study it more closely.

She pulled back in alarm and even shame as he broke the mood. Did Theo find the ugly scars as repulsive as she did? Was this his way of showing her that he couldn't face taking her to bed? She had never examined the damage as closely as he was doing. She had never been able to bring herself to the point where she could accept the full horror of her fate. She held her breath until he had finished his examination.

'The next couple of weeks are going to be very busy for me, Miranda. But when things quieten down I want you to agree to come with me and see another doctor.'

When she tried to explain that it would do no good, he laid a finger on her lips.

'You think a cure is impossible. You think no one can help you. I don't accept *impossible*, Miranda. I never have.'

Theo's voice was low, but fierce, and she could see how his business adversaries might shrink from it. 'You'd be wasting your time.' She held his stare.

Without breaking eye contact, he raised her hand to his lips. 'Don't tell me this isn't worth fighting for.'

She had to look away. It was the one battle she had always been frightened to face.

'I'm sorry if I've upset you, but—' Dipping his head, he looked her in the eyes. 'You may not know it, but your happiness is tied up in the damage to your hand. I'm going to make sure that you are set free to find happiness again.'

That same certainty and confidence fed Theo's success, Miranda realised. She could only hope it never turned into something harsher and more restrictive where she was concerned. If he tried to manipulate her it was the one thing that would split them apart.

'Why are you shivering? You need never be frightened again, Miranda, you are a Savakis now.'

Again the pride. Again the absolute certainty. But when he started unlacing her gown she couldn't hold on to the worries niggling at her—not with her senses under siege like this.

'Do you want me, Miranda?' he asked softly.

'You know I do...'

Yes, and she trusted him completely, Miranda realised, as Theo slipped the wedding gown from her shoulders. As it pooled on the ground she stepped out of it, naked now except for the shimmering silk chemise and tiny briefs she wore beneath.

Holding his gaze, she reached up and started unfastening the buttons on his traditional shirt. Her hands were trembling, and she had little dexterity at the best of times, but instead of growing impatient and trying to help her when he saw she was struggling Theo didn't interfere.

Her breath left her lungs in a rush as she pushed the soft

fabric aside. Theo was so beautiful she wanted to touch every part of him. His warm scent was an aphrodisiac that made her want to melt into him and lose herself.

She gasped when his hands moved to slip the dainty straps on her silk chemise from her shoulders, and when he eased the delicate garment over her breasts her arousal was evident to both of them. Her breasts seemed fuller, and were flushed pink around nipples that stood erect for his attention. She moaned softly at his first delicate touch, wondering if she would survive the sensation of firm thumb pads teasing her. 'Don't torture me…'

'I'll stop if you don't like it.'

'No…' Her nipples were straining towards him, growing taut and increasingly sensitive beneath each feathering touch, and then he moved to circling, before tugging gently with his thumb and forefinger.

'More?' he demanded softly, disposing of the chemise.

'Yes…oh, yes…'

Cupping her heavy breasts, he weighed them appreciatively while his thumbs worked steadily on her nipples. Rivers of sensation were streaming through her, and when he stopped she cried out with disappointment.

'Tell me what you want, Miranda.'

She couldn't believe Theo was asking her to become the architect of her own pleasure. She had never dreamed that a man might be capable of treading such an erotic path.

'You have to tell me exactly what you want me to do, Miranda, or I'll have to stop…'

'Touch me, Theo…stroke me…'

'Like this?'

She cried out with pleasure as he increased the pressure on her breasts.

'Or like this?'

Her mouth fell open as his searching hand found the source of her pleasure.

'Are you ready for me yet?'

He stroked and stroked again, delicately and persuasively, and all the time he watched her with dark, knowing eyes so full of promises. 'Yes…' She stared up at him, mutely begging him for release.

She hadn't expected him to drop to his knees, or to ease the flimsy briefs from her hips and bury his face between her thighs. She hadn't dreamed such extremes of sensation existed, and she sobbed with relief when after a brief kiss of homage she felt the rough scratch of his stubble on her thighs.

Theo's tongue was so bold, so demanding, and her legs were too weak to hold her now. She might have slipped to the floor without his strong arms supporting her.

Gasping for breath, she planted her hands on his shoulders and, rolling her head back, begged, 'Take me to bed, Theo… Take me now.'

For the first time in her life she felt the power of her sex, and as Theo carried her across the room and lowered her down onto the satin sheets she was ready for him.

She was like a flower whose petals were opening beneath him, Theo thought. She was everything he had hoped for and more. Dimitri was wrong. Life had no meaning, no purpose, without emotion, without someone to care for, someone to love. What a dynasty they would found together. Miranda would teach him how to care, and he would protect her with his life.

Allowing his clothes to drop to the floor, he heard her gasp. Half turning, he made sure he was angled away from her. The last thing he wanted to do now was frighten her. The urge to shield Miranda from harm was growing stronger by the moment. Whatever life held in store for both of them, he would do everything in his power to make her happy.

Slipping into bed beside her, he covered himself with the satin sheet and, smoothing a wayward strand of hair from her brow, demanded, 'Do you trust me now, Miranda?'

'I trust you completely…'

That was all he needed to hear. He relaxed and stretched out beside her. Her breathing was rapid and her eyes were almost black, with just a fine ring of jade to remind him of their colour. Pulling the sheet back, he relished every tiny change that marked the blossoming of her arousal: her swollen lips, her almost painfully erect nipples, and, most of all, the subtle undulation of her hips that called his attention to the source of her need.

Trailing his fingers lightly, so they barely touched her quivering frame, he brought them down from the hollow at the base of her neck, on between her breasts and then over the swell of her belly. But as her eyes widened with anticipation he brought his hand up again, and began idly toying with her breasts.

'Stop teasing me, Theo.'

'I thought you liked it?' He pretended surprise, but he saw how she squirmed with pleasure each time he cupped her firmly and chafed her puckered nipples with his thumb pads. 'More?' He knew how it turned her on to ask.

'Take me in your mouth…'

She angled her breast and spoke so softly it was almost a sigh. Then, reaching for him, she drew him down to suckle. She writhed beneath him while he pleasured her, but he made her wait until she begged, 'Theo, please! Don't make me wait any longer…'

Moving over her, he nudged her thighs apart, and was pleased when she opened herself even more for him. He caressed her intimately to be sure, and then was forced to take her mouth and hold on to his control, plunging his tongue deep instead of all the other things he wanted to do to her. Tasting her sweetness was a sharp reminder of how inexperienced she was…but then she arced towards him, forcing their bodies together, and he knew he was lost.

Holding her firmly, he made a single pass, feathering over her. She delivered the answer he had hoped for, drawing up her thighs even more as she choked out a single word. 'Yes…'

He made a second pass, and this time allowed the tip to catch inside her. She exhaled raggedly and held his gaze with half-shut sleepy eyes.

'Yes,' she breathed again, moving her hips in an attempt to take him deeper.

He resisted the temptation to follow her instructions. He would set the pace. He would choose the moment. And then she closed her eyes, relaxing completely in his arms in an attitude of complete trust, with one arm resting languidly above her head on the satin pillows.

But still he withdrew and made her wait. She was tender and innocent, and she was his…

He had underestimated his wife. Wrapping her hand around him, she made him gasp. The sensation was like nothing he had ever known before, and now Miranda was guiding him back, bringing him to where her hips were lifting from the bed.

He kissed her deeply, groaning as she tightened her hold on him. She made an insistent raw sound as he eased inside her, and then clung to him as if terrified he might change his mind. When he moved from side to side, settling himself inside her, she rose against him, closing her muscles round him to draw him deeper still.

His bride was perfect. Miranda was perfect. Nothing on earth could come between them now.

* * *

As Theo thrust inside her, Miranda wondered if she would survive the waves of pleasure washing over her. She had never dreamed there could be such extremes of sensation, and in that moment she lost all her inhibitions. Crying out, she allowed him to guide her with his strong hands, moulding her buttocks as she worked her hips in unison with his. Their lovemaking gathered pace until they were both lost, until she felt the breath gathering in her chest, the cry collecting in her throat…

Holding her in his arms, Theo urged her fiercely in his own tongue until her lips parted in a long, silent wail. She thrashed her head about, fighting off the moment, but as her throbbing muscles gripped him she screamed his name and they tumbled together over the edge of the abyss.

She came to in a state of complete relaxation. Her body felt as if it might float away. She turned her head to stare at Theo. He had collapsed on the pillows at her side and rolled away. Maybe he was asleep? She had no strength to find out. Her eyelids were so heavy…

'Theo?'

Waking slowly, Miranda realised it was morning and she was alone in the vast bed. Swinging her legs over the side, she searched for him, but their suite of rooms was empty. She checked the balcony too, and the bathroom, but there was no sign of her husband.

And they were at sea. But hadn't Theo said they would be spending their honeymoon on Kalmos?

After she'd showered, she slipped on one of the towelling robes hanging in the bathroom. Her wedding dress was still on the floor by the bed, where they had discarded it along with Theo's clothes.

Caressing it, she scooped everything up and laid the clothes straight, smiling as the events of the night came back to her.

Who would have guessed she had such an appetite? Theo had awoken a whirlwind. And who would have guessed he possessed the power to hold her nightmares at bay? Tension poured out of her in a sigh.

She found some slippers to match the robe on a shelf beside the bed, and was so impatient to see him again she didn't wait to dry her hair.

She found him seated at the table where they had been supposed to eat supper the previous evening. All signs of romance had been removed: the candles, the linen windbreakers. Now an awning cast shade across the table and he sat with a coffee cup in one hand and what looked like a report in the other. He was surrounded by documents and had his satellite phone within reach, Miranda noticed, grimacing.

He was too preoccupied to notice her padding up to him. 'Good morning,' she said brightly, resting her hands on his shoulders as she planted a kiss on his neck. 'Why didn't you wake me?'

He lifted his hand to silence her. 'Forgive me, I must read this…'

Miranda's smile died and she pulled her hands away from Theo's stiff, unyielding shoulders. She felt a chill, a premonition.

'Have some breakfast?' he suggested, flashing her the briefest smile.

Perhaps he was being discreet for the sake of the crew and she was overreacting? She glanced around, but they were alone.

'Don't you want any breakfast?' he pressed, without lifting his head from the papers he was studying.

'Yes, thank you. That would be nice.' She felt hurt and angry. There wasn't a word of endearment from him, not even a look.

'I had a place laid for you in case you woke up…' He

shrugged apologetically as he glanced round at all his business paraphernalia.

Her place at the table was as far away from him as possible. Maybe he was like this in the morning? How would she know? She didn't know him…and Theo clearly didn't know her either.

She made no fuss; just moved a stack of folders aside to make room for a place-setting closer to him, and when a steward appeared with a jug of orange juice she asked him, 'Would you mind bringing that chair over here for me?'

'Certainly, madam.'

'I'm sorry to be dressed like this,' she tried as an icebreaker once she had sat down. 'I don't have any clothes with me, as you know. If you'd warned me I would have packed a case. Goodness knows, it wouldn't have taken long…'

No response from Theo.

'I didn't realise we were going to sea. I thought you said our honeymoon was to be in Kalmos.'

Nothing.

She waited until the steward had disappeared down the companionway. 'Theo, is something wrong?'

'No, of course not. But I must read this.'

'On the morning after our wedding night?'

'This can't wait. I'm sorry.'

'I'm afraid it's going to have to wait.' Taking the document from his hands, she laid it aside. 'I haven't got any clothes with me; I don't know where we're going or what's going on. The least you can do is spare me a few minutes to explain.'

'You have to understand that you haven't married the boy next door, Miranda. I run a very complicated business, and I have to check each day to see which way the wind is blowing—'

'Well, I can tell you which way the wind is blowing in your

marriage, Theo!' She stood up. 'If you don't make space for me there's no point in our being married—'

'Don't talk like that!'

She had his full attention now. 'If you think I'm going to sit around waiting for you to fit me in between meetings, you're wrong. You promised me time. You said there would be all the time in the world for us to get to know each other. How can that be right, Theo, when you can't even find time for me today?'

As he reached for her she took a step back. 'Think about what I've said, Theo—think about it good and long. You have to decide if you want me, or if you want your wretched business more. Because if this is how it's going to be, I'm warning you now—you can't have both.'

CHAPTER NINE

MIRANDA was still shaking ten minutes later, in their state-room. She had expected—hoped—that Theo would come after her, to apologise and to reassure her. But there was no sign of him.

So was the fairytale over? It seemed so. She hugged her-self, wondering about the practicalities of leaving her husband in the middle of the ocean. It wasn't like stalking out of an apartment—she could hardly paddle back to shore. Theo's he-licopter was squatting like a big black bird on the helipad on the top deck, but she didn't imagine he would lend it to her so she could leave him.

And where could she go without clothes, without money, without even a satellite phone at her disposal to call for help? There really was no alternative. She had to go back on deck and sort this out with him.

'Kyrios Savakis is taking calls inside his office,' the steward informed her when she found Theo had left the breakfast table.

'I see.' So that was how much she meant to him! Thanking the steward, Miranda headed off.

When she found the right door she belted her robe a little more securely, knocked once, and walked straight in.

'Do come in, Miranda.'

Ignoring the sarcasm, she shut the door. 'I'd like five minutes of your time.'

He was seated behind a vast expanse of desk—which as far as Miranda was concerned was a welcome barrier between them. The blinds were drawn and his face was in shadow, as if he needed a blank canvas in which to think.

'Won't you sit down?' As he spoke, he switched on a desk lamp.

'I prefer to stand. Shall I draw the blinds?'

'As you wish.'

She did more than that; she opened the window, allowing the sea breeze to bring a refreshing draught inside the room. 'I asked you to make a decision about our marriage, Theo, and so far you haven't had the courtesy to let me know what you have decided.'

'Maybe I haven't decided how best to achieve a suitable balance in my life.'

'Indecision?' Her voice was sceptical. 'Not you, Theo.'

'What do I have to say to convince you that I love you, but that I run a very large and very complex business—a business that refuses to remain in suspension while I take a honeymoon with my bride?'

'You might have warned me that it would be like this!'

'So it's *you* who is having second thoughts, Miranda?'

'That's a low blow, Theo. Don't try and turn this around on me.'

She loved him so much that it hurt—but could she give up her free will, as well as all her own hopes for the future, to provide comfort in bed for a busy plutocrat? Was she to walk obediently at Theo's side and provide him with children as and when required? Was this what she had intended when she set out to rebuild her life? Was she destined to be a handy vessel, waiting for the blessing of his seed?

'I don't know what you had in mind when you married me, but I won't be your whore, Theo—'

He started as if she had slapped him. 'Don't use that language!'

'Why, Theo? Because it's a little too close to the truth? Do you get a kick out of inexperienced women who have everything to learn at your hands?'

'What women?' Theo was equally angry now. He leapt up and came angrily round the desk, grasping her shoulders. 'Don't sully what we have by even thinking such travesties about me!'

'Let me go,' she warned.

'No.'

She stood stiffly in his arms, averting her face when he spoke again. 'There is bound to be a period of readjustment—'

'Readjustment?' she said furiously, shaking him off. 'I'll say there is. You can't expect to make love to me all night and then ignore me in the morning because of business—because of *anything*. It's time to get your priorities straight, Theo, and think about the things that matter!'

And that was exactly what he had been doing; that was why he had woken up so early and why she had found him in a sombre mood. He had neglected Miranda for the best of reasons—because she had made him see what was important in life. He loved her, really loved her, and he hadn't thought himself capable of the emotion.

'Miranda, please. I love you—'

'And that makes everything better? I need *time* with you, Theo.'

'This isn't a normal time for me.' He battled with all the things he wanted to tell her but knew he couldn't. 'Please believe me when I say that if circumstances had been different I wouldn't have left you alone for a moment.'

'Then share your problems with me! Let me understand. I want to help you, Theo, but you have to let me in…'

How could he find the words to explain that Dimitri was fading, and that after a lifetime of indifference between them he wanted to go like a peacemaker and show the old man his bride. And not because it would guarantee him control of the Savakis shipping line, but because he was so proud of Miranda—because he wanted his grandfather to share in his happiness at the end.

Never having experienced love before, he hadn't known how it would affect him. It was as if everything that had been suppressed in him had suddenly come to the fore. But he couldn't risk it. Dimitri might say something, and Miranda's courage wasn't inexhaustible. Her belief that her life could be rebuilt had been the catalyst that had set him thinking, but did he want to destroy that belief and show her what their marriage looked like through Dimitri's eyes?

The truth was, he was locked into a deceit from which there was no escape. He hated himself for it, and that was why he had shut himself away. How could he look Miranda in the face when she had given herself to him so fully, so honestly? How could he look at her now without the spectre of the golden shares standing between them? She meant everything to him, but if she ever found out about the contract he had signed she would never trust him again. Was that the foundation upon which he hoped to found a dynasty?

'So you've nothing to say to me?'

She sounded so sad, and, drawing herself up, she shook her head in disappointment. 'If you can't share your life with me, Theo, I've got no place to be. Can't you see that? If silence is your answer you have to let me go—'

'No!'

'You have to. Or is your pride such that you can't bear to admit that you've made a mistake?'

'I haven't made a mistake.'

'Then why can't you confide in me?'

He hesitated. 'Because it's confidential.'

'Confidential?' As she stared at him he felt more pain than triumph as understanding coloured her gaze. 'Then why on earth didn't you say so?'

His throat was so tight he could only manage a noncommittal sound to go with his shrug.

'Oh, Theo…' She touched his face. 'We're both novices at this. Forgive me?'

Seizing her hand, he pressed it to his lips. 'So you've changed your mind about leaving me?'

'What do you think?'

'Now it's my turn to ask you to forgive me. I've been alone too long. I can't see any further than the problems in the business. They blinded me to how you might be feeling.'

'Then leave all this—' she gestured round his office '—and be with me now. Otherwise you had better set me ashore with some clothes, and I'll be a castaway.'

Her humour made him feel worse than ever, and as she pressed her lips together in a rueful smile he knew he had to come up with a better strategy. 'All this can wait,' he told her, pushing the documents on his desk aside. 'You're more important to me than any business deal.'

'Just be sure you mean it, Theo.' She turned serious. 'I don't want to make another mistake, and I don't want to be pushed around by anyone—not even you. I know the consequences that can have. If I'd hadn't let myself be pressured into getting in that car when I should have waited for my taxi, *this* might never have happened.'

His mouth dried when she raised her damaged arm to make the point, but he followed through with the lighter mood she had set before. 'I'm not calling for a taxi, so you're stuck with me. You're everything I want, Miranda.'

But as he heard the words he was saying and looked into her eyes he wondered if it were possible to despise himself more. Deceiving Miranda about his motives for marrying her would keep their marriage alive for now—but at what cost?

Perhaps this was his punishment for breaking every one of Dimitri's rules. Miranda was artistic, and perhaps fleetingly he had been guilty of seeing her as a worthy cause—someone who might be grateful for his attention—but he was over that. She had taught him more than he could ever repay her for.

'Come on.' Walking to the door before she could see the emotion in his eyes, he held it open. 'Let's have that talk.'

They exchanged reassurances over coffee, and talked on through lunch when an easy mood was restored.

'You'd better find me some clothes to wear,' she reminded him. 'Or did you imagine you were going to keep me in bed for the whole trip?'

He kissed her brow and was relieved to hear her laugh. 'There's a whole wardrobe of clothes waiting for you in your dressing room.' He gestured down the deck towards their stateroom. 'I wanted to surprise you.'

'Theo, you're full of surprises,' she mocked him gently.

'Should I have them moved to another stateroom, or are we still married?' He slanted a glance at her; outwardly smiling, inwardly tense.

'Still married.'

He made a sound of deep contentment.

Their reunion was explosive. Having stripped away her fear of sex, Theo had awakened a hunger in Miranda she had no idea how to control. Fortunately Theo was tireless and inventive, and had plenty of ideas when it came to channelling her energies.

What was happening to her? Miranda wondered as she got dressed again. Adrenaline was still pumping through her veins; she couldn't get enough of him. She had always shied away from involvement and hadn't been looking for love when love had found her.

It must be some really bad flaw in her character that always made her question anything that seemed to be too good to be true. For once she should just lie back and accept that her marriage to Theo was that good.

Emily had always been the more confident twin—the twin who took the lead, led her class, seized opportunities. Ten minutes might be nothing in the scheme of things, but when it came to which twin was born first it had made all the difference. Even at the music *conservatoire* Miranda had been content to stay in the background until winning a major competition had made that impossible.

And then had come the accident and a whole new set of rules. They had all been special at college, all hothouse flowers, and it had bred a complacency that hadn't prepared her for life after the crash. If she wasn't a world-class musician, then what was she?

Theo had answered that question. She was a woman who had survived a devastating trauma and was ready to move forward to the next stage of her life. Take the violin away and she was still out there fighting; take her self-belief away and she was nothing.

Trusting Theo had brought her life into sharper focus. Their chance meeting had changed her life. She mustn't let her fears sabotage her future.

Tilting her chin, she adjusted the collar on a beautifully tailored shirt she had discovered in her dressing room after his prompt. Their marriage was safe, their love like a white light blazing steadily between them. It was more than she could have hoped for when she agreed to be his wife. Theo was the air she breathed, the force that had given her life meaning again. He was everything to her now.

'What's that?' Miranda stared at the documents Theo had laid out in front of him on the desk in his office.

'I've drawn up a contract—I'm afraid it's longhand, but I thought it would be something that might reassure you...'

'I don't need anything else to reassure me.'

'You may do—you never know. One day when you're feeling down—for no reason,' he added hastily, adding a smile. 'Why don't you sign? It would make me feel better if you do.'

It was hard to refuse him anything, but if she had learned one thing during her short career it was: Don't sign anything until you've checked it over thoroughly. And she shouldn't close her mind to Theo's moods. Okay, he was in a stressful business, but they had a long way to go yet.

Miranda chewed down on her lip, hesitating. Theo's eyes were half closed as he sat watching her. He wore a similar expression when they were making love. But was good sex enough to hold a marriage together?

Theo had answered that question with a contract. A man thing, Miranda realised, smiling inwardly. As far as men were concerned anything and everything could be put to bed with a contract. 'I'd like to read it before I sign.'

'Of course.' He pushed it across the desk.

She studied it. 'What's this lump sum?' Pointing to the relevant paragraph, she pushed it back to him.

Scanning the item briefly, he looked up. 'That's not a lump sum; it's your monthly allowance. *Calendar* month,' he stressed, as if that were a limitation she must consider.

'Why, that's...' She had been about to say *ridiculous*, because the sum was extraordinary, but remembering the world Theo came from, she amended it to, '…reasonable.'

'I'm glad you think so. So, will you sign?' Uncapping a fountain pen, he held it out to her.

'I haven't quite finished reading it yet.' Her mind was racing with possibilities for the future, and various ways she might use the money.

This was a surprise to Theo. He had expected hesitation, had expected she would be a little bit daunted, but instead Miranda appeared to be coolly accepting the fact that her monthly allowance would be roughly equivalent to most people's annual salary. He had to admit he admired her style.

'I don't like this.'

Instinctively he bridled as she pointed to a passage. 'I beg your pardon?' No one found fault with a contract *he* had approved, let alone one he had drawn up himself.

'I can't be called upon at your whim, Theo.' She passed the sheet back to him. 'We will *both* keep diaries, and then we can consult *each other* regarding our availability.'

'Very well.' He could feel a muscle working in his jaw.

'And I'd like you to fax the contract to my sister Emily, for her to take a look at.'

'Your sister?'

'She's a barrister, civil law, and though she married a prince she is still in practice. This kind of thing is right up her street.'

This kind of thing? Was she referring to their marriage contract? As their looks clashed and held, Theo found himself on the back foot. He wasn't happy with the notion of outsiders intruding on his most private business, even if that outsider was Miranda's twin.

'And there's one more thing I'd like written into this.'

'What?' He cut across her abruptly, and then reined back, surprised at the surge of emotion he felt at her challenge.

'What's missing?' He managed to lower his voice, but found himself shaking his head as if denying the possibility that he might have overlooked so much as a comma.

'*I* decide what I do with my monthly allowance.'

He relaxed. 'Of course.' Shopping was a harmless occupation. And it would give her something to do when he was busy.

'Good. I'm glad we've got that straight, Theo, because I'm going to be using the money to set up scholarships for promising music students who couldn't otherwise afford the best tuition. I will also do some teaching myself, and of course I will sit on the committee that auditions prospective candidates.'

Theo sat back, feeling a mixture of emotions. He was surprised, of course, and a little put out that being his wife wasn't enough for Miranda, but above all he was exhilarated to see her so recovered emotionally—to the point where she was making plans for the future. And why was he surprised? That was Miranda, always bouncing back, always with an original take on life.

But he had to pull her up on one point. 'So you won't be partial?'

'What do you mean, partial?'

She was defensive, and he guessed she had expected him to say categorically no. 'I mean you can hardly cherry-pick the best students and then award them the scholarships. You must remain impartial if you want other teachers to subscribe to your scheme—or did you intend to teach all these gifted students by yourself? How about setting up a trust, with a board of trustees to administer the programme?'

'That's a great idea,' Miranda admitted, thrilled that Theo was getting on board. Music was her forte, but business just wasn't her thing. 'Okay, perhaps you could help me?'

'Me?'

'Why not you?' She stared at him. Necessity was the

mother of invention, and she was going to need some professional help to bring her ideas to fruition. Theo was the best, and he was cheap too, under the principle 'keep it in the family and he'll work for nothing'—which in turn left more money for the students. 'Well?' she pressed.

'I'd have to think about it. I'm a very busy man, Miranda.'

The shadow of Theo's business passed over them once again, showing that she was right not to weaken. Their marriage would have to be an equal partnership or it wouldn't survive. 'Too busy to work with me, Theo?'

'I said I'll think about it.'

'Then put the cap back on your pen and think about it while I take this contract away to read through it quietly. When I've finished I'll let you know, and then we can fax it to my sister Emily in Ferara.'

Rising politely from his seat, Theo granted her a faintly mocking bow.

The reply came through from Emily almost immediately. Fortunately she had been in her office at the palace when the fax arrived.

As Theo handed Miranda the reply, she pictured the scene in Ferara. Emily would have been tearing her hair out after scanning the document and realising it was a post-nuptial agreement rather than a pre-nuptial one. She would have erupted before she got down to studying it closely. This supposition was borne out by the fact that Emily had penned a swift response by hand, not even bothering to type it out first. Written in her twin's uncompromising script, the words positively vibrated with frustration.

Why the hell didn't you ask me to look at this BEFORE you married him?
Em.

There weren't even any kisses by her name, though Emily had underlined the abbreviation—as if there could be any mistake, Miranda thought, biting back her smile.

'And here's another one,' Theo informed her with a heavy sigh, leaning back on his chair to retrieve a second fax. 'Also from Ferara.'

Miranda shot him a warning glance. His irony only made him more attractive, and she wanted to keep a clear head. Taking the fax from him, she turned her back to concentrate.

And don't expect me to read this contract in a hurry. I don't sit around waiting for you to do something silly, you know. I do work. And how are you, by the way? Are you all right? For goodness' sake, let me know.

'May I?' She turned around again and glanced at the pen tray on his desk.

He dipped his head. 'Be my guest.'

Choosing a corner away from him, she wrote:

I'm fine. Please don't worry about me. Marriage to Theo is rather more complicated than I had expected, that's all. Tell me what you think when you come to the blessing!

And then, as an afterthought she added:

Sorry for all this! M xxx

'Will you send it for me?' she asked, turning to Theo. He held out his hand.

She waited until it was safely dispatched and then turned to go.

'You'd better take these with you. I've no wish to intrude.'
He gave her the faxed copies.

'I'll shred them.'

'So?' Theo said at last, when the shredder fell silent.

'So?' Miranda repeated.

'Are you going to give me a clue? Did Emily give you her
first impression?'

Oh, yes, she had! And who could blame Em for feeling the
way she did, when Theo's handwritten contract had arrived
on her desk within a few short days of her learning that her
twin was about to be married to a stranger? Shock, horror, incredulity—those wouldn't even begin to cover Emily's reaction. And that was before she got round to indignation and
hysterical laughter, Miranda guessed.

'She said she would read it through and let me have her
thoughts at the blessing,' she said carefully.

'I want an answer now. Or at least by close of business
today.'

Theo kept his voice low, but he might as well have
thumped the desk. Miranda bristled. She wasn't another of
his business assets, to be quickly dealt with and filed away.
'Close of business?'

'Yes.'

'Well, you can't have it. My sister's very busy.'

'And I'm not?'

Theo controlled his impatience with difficulty. The contract
had to be signed. The documents he had been poring over the
morning after their wedding had come from Dimitri's lawyers.
They reminded him that, according to the instructions in his
grandfather's will, he must remain married to Miranda for at
least thirty days for the share transfer to take place. The contract he had drawn up bound Miranda to their marriage for
double that time. Naturally the true purpose of the agreement

would never come out, and in the unlikely event that she balked at sixty days he had sugared the pill with a huge cash incentive and every safeguard he could put in place for her. No one in their right mind would refuse to sign.

It was another step on the road to his goal, and helped to salve his conscience as well. He had thought the contract would give her something to mull over, something to get excited about—something to keep her busy while he took the helicopter and made his peace with Dimitri. This last gesture meant a lot to him, and he owed his change of heart to Miranda. But he would go alone. He couldn't risk any last-minute complications...

'Why are you in such a hurry for my answer, Theo?'

'Such a hurry?' Repeating Miranda's words with a garnish of incredulity, he adopted an affronted expression. 'I am making over a king's ransom to you, and yet you are reluctant to sign?'

She turned her face away, as if she needed a moment to put her thoughts into words. 'That's very generous of you, but this is our honeymoon. Must it always come down to business for you, Theo?'

She was right, and he wished at that moment that it wasn't so, but money, business, they were the only things he truly understood. 'I'm sorry. I thought the contract would be like a wedding gift—a reassurance for you...' He sighed as if he were the one who was hurt. However bad it made him feel, on this occasion he had to manipulate the situation.

'It is very generous. Perhaps too generous, Theo. But I can't push Emily into reading it for me right away.'

Why not? He curbed his impatience, knowing it wouldn't help his case. 'Perhaps you could send her a fax expressing your impatience, and mention that project you have in mind?' She hesitated, but he could see he had hit the right spot.

'That seems reasonable...'

Handing her a pen, he stood over her while she quickly wrote a note.

'Well, that's done,' she said, after he had faxed it to Ferara. 'Now all we can do is wait.'

'I disagree,' he said, drawing her into his arms.

CHAPTER TEN

MAKING love was all-consuming for both of them, Theo reflected as he kicked the door of the stateroom shut behind them. Would they make it to the bed this time? It seemed unlikely. They were already wrapped around each other as if every inch of their bodies must be in contact for them to survive. Clothes were discarded with indecent haste. Miranda was insatiable, and he…he just wanted to forget.

Gathering her into his arms, he locked her legs around his waist and carried her the few steps to the long console table that ran against the wall. Sweeping some papers aside, he lowered her down.

She yelped as her naked flesh came into contact with the frigid marble, but when he moved in for a kiss, murmuring endearments, trying to take it slow, she curled her fingers around his neck and dragged him down to her. As their tongues clashed in a prelude to the greater intimacy they were about to share he slid his hands up her thighs, and when she moaned encouragement he drew his tongue along the full swell of her bottom lip, keeping their mouths touching so that he could feel as well as hear the little cry she always made when he entered her.

She gasped, and, reaching for him, clutched his buttocks

to force him on, but he drew back, making her wait. 'Don't be so impatient.'

'Oh, please, Theo…'

It was tempting to follow her desperate command, but so much better for both of them if he directed the pace. 'Not yet,' he husked against her lips.

'I can't wait,' she wailed, stabbing her fingers into him.

He was so engorged he thought he might hurt her, and proceeded slowly, easing himself into her little by little. Throwing back her head in triumph, she worked her hips urgently to draw him deeper.

'Theo, please…'

He moved more firmly, keeping the rhythm slow. He loved to give her pleasure, loved to see her flushed and quivering with excitement. It made him want to give her more. He upped the pace. It made him want to give her everything…

He waited until the first climax had subsided, and then, lifting her into his arms he carried her over to the bed. He was still deep inside her, and she was still begging him for more. 'Soon,' he promised. 'The moment we get there…'

'Theo,' she sighed, as he settled her down on the satin sheets.

'What do you want, baby?' Her eyes were half closed, and her breathing through damp, parted lips was soft and rapid.

'Kiss me…'

'How could he resist? Dipping his head, he kissed her tenderly on the lips.

'Kiss me properly.'

He smiled, and tried again.

'Mmm, that's better,' she said at last when he let her go.

He loved to see the effect of his restraint. It was always the same. She responded so eagerly. Her nipples were almost painfully erect, and her breasts were like two perfect globes, all of which demanded his attention. Cupping her breasts, he made her gasp, and that gasp soon turned to a whimper as he began to chafe each perfect bud with his thumb pad.

'I want you now. I don't want to wait…'

Her voice was soft and insistent as her eyes implored him. She was exquisite, sweetly scented, and warm beneath his lips. And as he suckled and tugged and heard her sob with pleasure he knew that all he wanted was Miranda, and that he had to make this marriage work.

She had been foolish to doubt him. Theo had taken every one of her doubts and obliterated them with a kiss. She loved him so deeply there were no words to describe how she felt. It was already impossible to imagine what her life had been without him…without *this*, she knew, as he thrust into her again. Would she ever get enough of him? It didn't seem possible.

When Theo left her to tie up some loose ends Miranda took a long bath to consider her thoughts about the scholarship scheme. She was in a ferment of new ideas, and Theo had promised to discuss them with her over dinner.

After drying her hair, she dressed with particular care, making full use of the beautiful selection of clothes and accessories she had found in her dressing room. Leaving her hair loose, she had applied the minimum of make-up and just a spritz of scent. When she had boosted her student income by working as a cabaret singer, mask-like make-up had been *de rigueur*—to the point where she'd felt naked without it; she hated it now.

She wanted to make the extra effort because they had never been closer. She wanted to show Theo how happy he made her, and how she wanted to play a full role in his life as he would in hers. For the first time since their hasty wedding she felt like his wife.

And now she was ready, Miranda decided, as she examined her reflection in the mirror. Goodness knew what Theo saw in her, when he could have anyone, but she would stand by him now through anything—everything.

Remembering his caution that the Savakis equivalent to a lottery win would be delivered to her door every calendar month, rather than every four weeks, she smiled. Didn't he know how that sounded to someone who had been prepared to work for the minimum wage? Twelve payments each year instead of thirteen, when each of those payments was in the stratosphere? Were people really so rich, so distanced from reality?

But she was one of those people now, Miranda remembered, and with wealth such as the Savakis family possessed came a scale of responsibility she had never encountered before. It made her all the more determined to make good use of the money. She would remember her roots too, and how luck had played such a huge part in her life. Without her brother-in-law's gift of a priceless violin she would never have been able to enjoy her short-lived career, and now she was in a position to extend that same opportunity to someone else. Money couldn't buy happiness, but it could open doors and enhance the prospects of the type of student she had in mind. Theo's monthly allowance was an unexpected gift, but she would grab it with both hands—even if one of those hands was pretty useless.

With a wry grin Miranda realised she hadn't felt this good since before the accident—or maybe ever. Without even knowing it Theo had restored something vital in her life; she had a cause to champion, as well as the chance to give something back.

She found him leaning on the rail, staring out across to sea. Climbing the last few steps of the companionway, she felt a new tension building as he turned and they stared at each other. The connection between them was powerful and unique.

They stared at each other in silence for a few moments, and she knew that he appreciated the trouble she had taken with her appearance. Theo didn't stare as some men might, as if she were a product they were evaluating and comparing with the rest. When Theo looked at her he made her feel like the only woman in the world. And he had taken the same amount of trouble, as if he had guessed she would choose a formal outfit from the selection in her wardrobe.

The gown was a simple fall of blue-grey silk, and she had draped a beautiful beaded shawl around her shoulders—but only to protect her against the unpredictable breeze that could spring up on the sea at night. Thanks to Theo, she was no longer so self-conscious about her injuries.

'Are you hungry?'

It was an innocent question, but Miranda still had to smother the smile tugging at her lips. The last time Theo had asked her that same question the food his chef had prepared for them had gone to waste. 'I need to eat,' she agreed cautiously.

'I need to eat too,' he assured her. 'I need to build up my strength.'

'Do you?' She feigned alarm.

With a wicked grin, he linked her arm through his and strolled with her to the table that had been set for them beneath the stars.

Miranda couldn't help reflecting that Theo was a very sensual man, which was a world apart from being a sexual athlete. But it was impossible to be in his company without at least considering how long it would be before he took her back to bed...

'We can't disappoint my chef a second time,' he murmured,

as if her thoughts were an open book to him. Briefly locking glances, they sat down. 'Though you do make it hard for me,' he added, 'because you look particularly beautiful tonight.' Raising her damaged hand to his lips, he kissed it in a way that made every part of her feel beautiful.

The table was laid with glittering crystal and a wealth of silverware on top of a fine white damask cloth. A dozen candles flickered in an exquisite Art Deco candelabrum, and Miranda thought the indolent pose of the figure gracing the stem the most erotic example of the silversmith's art she had ever seen.

'Exquisite, isn't she?' Theo murmured, noticing her interest.

'You're very lucky to have such things.'

He held her gaze, and suddenly Miranda was wondering if she was the most recent addition to his collection. Miranda Weston, off-the-shelf-bride, with her short-lived, if glorious musical career—something of a curiosity. It irritated her to discover that the insecurity was always lurking ready to pounce, but she couldn't hold back now. 'Why did you remain unmarried and then settle on me a matters of hours after we met, Theo?'

'Have you never heard of love at first sight?'

Miranda smiled, and Theo saw that she had relaxed, but her question had given him a jolt. Her bluntness was extraordinary, but of course that was one of the things he liked most about her. Would he tell the truth? No. How could he, when the truth was that he had needed a bride, and Miranda Weston, attractive and vulnerable, had happened along at the right moment? She would find the truth, that he had indeed fallen in love with her, just a little later, impossible to believe if he revealed the facts behind their hasty marriage.

'Ah—vichyssoise. My favourite chilled soup.' He straightened up with relief as the steward served them. 'Please thank the chef for me, will you, Marco?'

'Certainly, sir.'

'Champagne?' he suggested, turning to Miranda.

'That would be lovely.'

As she smiled into his eyes he wished he could tell her that the helicopter was fuelled, the flight plan filed, and that he would be taking off for the Savakis stronghold to see Dimitri as soon as they finished dinner. But he couldn't bring himself to break the mood, and there was too much at stake to risk upsetting Miranda and throwing yet another difficulty into the mix.

Miranda was glad Theo didn't ply her with wine. He didn't drink at all, she noticed, preferring to keep a clear head. But he did insist on feeding her morsels of food—food she couldn't resist any more than she could resist the expression in his eyes. The touch of his fingertips each time they accidentally brushed against her mouth was electrifying, and she almost rubbed her lips away with the linen napkin in an attempt to reduce their sensitivity.

'What's this?' she said, when the steward brought a low burner to the table and lit the flame. How many courses must they sit through before they could retire to their stateroom? Wicked thoughts, but she couldn't help herself. 'I thought we'd finished the meal?'

'Not until we've tasted my chef's *pièce de résistance*. Why? Are you in a hurry to get somewhere?'

She confined her answer to a look.

'I must do all the work now,' Theo informed her coolly, shrugging off his jacket.

'Dirty work?' she teased. A flick of each wrist was all it took to ditch his cufflinks, and he rolled back his sleeves.

And then a fresh fruit platter arrived: strawberries, mango, pear, pineapple and crunchy juicy apple slices, all of them ready to dip into warm chocolate sauce.

'Oh…' Miranda groaned. This was going to be very dirty

work indeed. And how was she supposed to behave in front of the crew when chocolate was dripping down her chin and Theo was catching it on his finger and sucking it clean?

The chocolate fondue had been a masterstroke. He was glad it had worked, relieved to see her so relaxed. This was their honeymoon, after all, and she deserved some fun. If the latest communication from Dimitri's doctor was to be believed, the fun was all but over for both of them. He didn't speak, because he didn't want to encourage questions. He was content to sit and wait for his co-pilot's signal.

As they sipped coffee Miranda wished the night could last for ever. It was so peaceful out on the ocean, with only the stars to keep them company and the sound of water breaking beneath the bow. She felt so close to Theo without the need for words. But when the steward returned with fresh coffee, she reached out with her damaged hand and clumsily knocked her cup over.

'Don't worry.' Theo waved the steward away. 'Here—let me pour you another cup. It's not important,' he insisted when she tried to mop up the mess. 'How did your injury happen, anyway? You never told me the whole story.'

She was unprepared for his directness, and her heart lurched at his mention of the accident. The feeling was as unpleasantly familiar as her nightmares.

She had locked the door in her mind on some horrible secrets, but as Theo continued to hold her gaze Miranda knew he wouldn't be fobbed off with any flimsy excuse. 'It happened after a concert, when I was still buoyed up on adrenaline and champagne. Unfortunately, the man who gave me a lift was in the same state. If only I'd been thinking clearly, I'd have taken account of the fact that he was drunk…I must have thought I was invincible.'

'People frequently do think that after a drink.'

'I should have waited for a taxi, I know.' She grimaced. 'It sounds so lame now, so obvious.'

'The lead-up to an accident always does. Otherwise we'd all know how to avoid them, wouldn't we?'

'Don't make allowances for me, Theo.' Her face tensed. 'Someone died. The driver was killed because of me.'

'But how could that be your fault? You said he was drunk.'

'Yes, he was. But—' She stopped, biting her lip. 'I distracted him.'

'How? Who was he?'

'He was my professor at the music *conservatoire*.' She sighed. 'There were two men, my teacher and my manager, and after the accident it became clear that both of them had been using me for their own reasons. My teacher had wanted to keep me to himself, lock me away like the heroine in *Phantom of the Opera*. He was a control freak.'

'And your manager?'

She smiled bitterly. 'After the accident, when I was no longer a meal ticket for him as a classical violinist, he tried to sell my "tragic story" to the tabloids.'

'I imagine you loved that?'

'I hated it.' She said the words fiercely under her breath, her mind a million miles from him.

'And your teacher died? That must have been devastating.' There was something wrong here, he knew it. He sensed she was hiding something, and was suddenly filled with an irrational fear. What was it? What was keeping her apart from him?

Coming to, she focused on his face. 'The whole experience was devastating. I was grateful to both of them for building my career, but I didn't want to be owned by them or manipulated by them. And then one died because of me, and the other betrayed me.'

She seemed so frank, yet something was still niggling at the back of his mind. 'How did your family take the news of the accident?'

'My family?' Miranda hesitated. She hadn't told them everything. How could she? 'They…' She could never tell lies to her family.

'They do know?' Theo pressed.

'Of course they know.'

'Everything? The full implication of what has happened to you? The fact that you will never play the violin on a concert platform again?'

'Of course. Theo, please.' She saw him looking at her as if he knew how raw her wounds were—but he couldn't know. 'Oh, the steward's here!' Leaning forward, she distracted Theo, welcoming the interruption.

'Excuse me, sir, but this fax has arrived for Kyria Savakis.'

'The royal crest of Ferara!' Miranda exclaimed as the steward passed it to her. 'Yes, it's from Emily,' she said after checking it. 'Do you mind?' Clutching the fax, she left the table.

Theo waited tensely, his dark gaze locked onto Miranda's back as she stopped a few feet away from him. He might have known Emily would drop everything the instant she'd received the handwritten contract. That was what was missing in *his* life—family members to rely on. There was an invisible bond between Miranda and her twin that even Miranda's absence had been unable to break. Emily probably had Alessandro's troops on standby right now, ready to fly out and execute a rescue mission.

He envied his wife's deep bond with her family. It was something he could never buy. After his parents had been killed in their light aircraft he had been raised in Dimitri's household, where a succession of highly paid professionals had overseen his upbringing and education. Dimitri had remained a sinister, shadowy figure, his only virtue in the eyes of a boy growing up the beautiful women he wore on his arm like so many bangles...

No, family was something he didn't know a great deal about. Before Miranda business had been his only passion; it responded to his control and grew ever stronger beneath his direction. It was the one unwavering point in his life—without it, what would he be?

Glancing up at Miranda, Theo felt another stab of envy. She had half turned towards him as she double-checked the fax again, and her pent-up excitement told him she was back, at least symbolically, in the bosom of the family to which she belonged. That closeness contrasted starkly with his own life to date.

But if he was nothing without his business, what did his future hold without Miranda?

CHAPTER ELEVEN

EMILY'S fax was like a comfort blanket after Theo's insistence that she tell him about the accident. He had been right to attempt to draw it out of her. It was the proverbial pus from a wound—the tragic death, the devastating consequences brought on by her own foolishness and two men's determination to manipulate another human being. But that didn't make it any easier to relive.

Wanting to share the news from Emily, she turned to go back to him. But the same steward had returned and appeared to be confiding an urgent message.

Miranda's heart thumped ominously when Theo shot up from the table. Meeting her gaze, he excused himself with the briefest nod.

His face was so bleak it frightened her. She stood motionless, watching him disappear in the direction of his office, still with Emily's fax clutched to her chest. She told herself to relax. Whatever had happened, Theo would deal with it. She would return to the table and wait for him.

The steward brought fresh coffee, and even some warm towels for her to refresh her hands after the messy pudding. But there was only so long she could sit counting stars. She had to go and see if she could do anything to help. She had just pushed her chair back from the table when he returned.

'You must forgive me, Miranda…'

She could tell he didn't want to sit down. He was tense and distracted, his face a grim mask. She stood up and tried to take his hand. 'Theo, what's happened?'

'My grandfather has passed away.'

'Oh, Theo, I'm so sorry—'

'I must return to the Savakis compound immediately.'

The Savakis compound? That didn't sound very inviting. 'Of course.' She could see he was sparking with impatience. 'I'll do anything I can to help you.' An image of her parents' small, cosy home flashed into Miranda's mind. She couldn't let him go alone. 'I'm coming with you.'

'Of course you'll come with me.'

Theo's voice was fierce, but she made allowances. Family was something she understood. He was devastated, but she would be there for him.

'Can you be ready quickly?'

'Of course.' Her mind raced. 'If you have a small suitcase I can borrow?'

'Borrow?' He stared at her as if she were a stranger. 'I'm sure the steward will find something for you. Look, there isn't time for a long-winded discussion, Miranda. Go to the stateroom and make a start.'

'If it's easier for you to go without me—'

'Without you?' He stared at her as if she was mad. 'Out of the question!'

Theo's face was pale beneath his tan—pale and tense. She had only wanted to reassure him, not add to his anguish.

'The helicopter will be ready to fly in fifteen minutes,' he said.

'The helicopter? Theo…' But he had already turned to go.

'There should be a black suit in your dressing room. Make sure you bring it,' he tossed over his shoulder.

She was already shaking, already quivering with the deep

and irrational fear of flying that had never eased, no matter how many times she took to the air. And now Theo was asking her to sit in a Plexiglas bubble and be held in the air by whirling cricket bats?

She had to do this…for him. 'How long will we be away?' she called after him, trying to focus her mind on what to pack.

'As long as it takes. Now, go!'

His commanding gesture took her by surprise, but she had to remember that this was a family bereavement—and it was also the first time she had been called upon to stand at his side. She had to put her fears aside, and, however brusque Theo's manner, she understood. She was his wife, and it was her duty to support him. He had obviously been very close to his grandfather, and must be feeling guilty for being away on his honeymoon at such a time. Sometimes life could be very cruel.

The helicopter ride was everything Miranda had dreaded. To make it worse, although Theo chose not to fly the aircraft himself, he sat next to the pilot—so she didn't even have his reassuring strength to cling on to. She sat as close as she could to him in the seat behind, trying not to vomit as the wretched machine sucked her stomach up with it into inky nothingness.

Theo must have given the pilot instructions to break all air speed records, Miranda gathered as they bounced through some bone-shaking turbulence. She was sure her face was white as her stomach turned over, but even then she sensed Theo was willing the aircraft to go faster if it could.

'Will it take long for us to get to your grandfather's home?' She had to ask. She had to know how long it would take. But Theo couldn't hear with his headphones on, so she had to lean forward and touch his neck.

'What do you want?' He frowned as he turned to look at her.

'Will it be much longer?' She hoped he didn't hear her voice quiver.

'I'm sorry.' His face softened, and, reaching out, he stroked her hair. 'This is an ordeal for you. Forgive me. I have so much on my mind—'

'Please, don't apologise.' She cut him off, hoping she had succeeded in masking her terror. 'I understand, Theo. You don't have to say anything.'

'Unless the weather closes in we should be there in under the hour.' With a smile of reassurance, he turned away.

Of course he was preoccupied; apart from missing his grandfather's last hours, he had a funeral to arrange and relatives to console. She had never considered Theo's relatives before, Miranda realised, her tension easing fractionally as her mind turned to practical matters. She had no idea if the Savakis clan was as large and loving as Spiros and Agalia's extended family, or a small, close unit like her own. But, however many people arrived to celebrate Dimitri's life, she was ready to help. She was free from any emotional entanglement and therefore could attend to practical matters, like food and who would sleep where, while Theo spent time with people who would undoubtedly be as distressed as he was.

It was a woman thing, Miranda realised. Theo was wounded, and her natural instinct was to care for him. And on top of that they had a strong relationship. When one of them was down, the other pulled them up.

Taking Emily's fax out of her pocket, she curled her fingers round it like a talisman. She couldn't wait to share the contents with Theo, but it would have to keep until a more appropriate time. She didn't need to read it again to remember the words Emily had written.

*They say lightning doesn't strike twice in the same place.
I think it just did! Where did you find him? Love Em xxx*

The moment they climbed out of the helicopter Theo was surrounded by men in dark suits who barely acknowledged
Miranda's presence. Theo was dressed formally too, as she was,
but he looked different somehow—different and forbidding.

Her legs were still shaking so badly it took her a moment
to regroup and chase after him. She was relieved when he
stopped and, holding up his hands to silence everyone, turned
back to look for her.

'Miranda…' He held out his hand.

But only as a signal that she should stop dawdling,
Miranda discovered, when she hurried towards him and he
started off again.

The huge building they were approaching looked like
something out of a Gothic horror movie. Every window was
shuttered and not a glimmer of light escaped, as if Dimitri
Savakis had wanted to shut out the world. She couldn't help
imagining the transformation that might occur if lights were
blazing and there were people buzzing back and forth behind
the shuttered panes…

No, money couldn't buy everything, and here was the
proof. The Savakis ancestral home might be grand, but it was
soulless, and even an energetic imagination like her own
couldn't stretch far enough to picture a family living there.

By the time they reached the entrance Miranda was feeling a deep and irrational sense of dread. She put it down to
the fact that beyond the house she had spotted a wire fence,
and even lookout posts. From the warning signs she gathered
the fence was electrified. If this was what the super-rich called
home, the appeal was lost on her.

As vast arched doors swung open, the men striding in

front of her stopped abruptly and she almost bumped into them. Theo was waiting politely to one side, allowing her to cross the threshold in front of him. Tipping her chin, she walked in.

Her first footsteps sent an echo spinning round a vast marble hallway, and in her peripheral vision she was aware that liveried servants were bowing low. Beyond that, there was silence. Irrationally, she longed for a hug, or a sound—any sound. But her introduction to the Savakis compound was about as cosy as walking into an airport terminal building…though this one had mammoth chandeliers, and what might have been antique French furnishings. At the far end there was a grand sweeping staircase, and lined up in front of it a motionless group of about thirty men and women, all wearing the same unrelieved black.

Miranda's stomach did a fast loop. None of them was looking at her, she realised; they were all staring at Theo, as if he had brought with him the very air they had to breathe.

'The relatives,' he explained, dipping forward to murmur in her ear, and then, placing a hand beneath her arm, he steered her forward.

It was a receiving line of black crows. Not a nice way to feel about your husband's family, Miranda reflected as she moved down the line, but it was an apt description for this group. Keeping her own face schooled to neutrality, she murmured a few words to each, searching for a single pair of eyes holding sorrow or sympathy, anything other than shrewd calculation. There wasn't a single pair. Instead she detected the barely suppressed excitement that sometimes—horribly—accompanied a death, when people started to fathom what it might mean to them in terms of financial gain.

How terrible it must have been for Theo to grow up in such a place and with such people—and to be amongst them now,

when he had just lost his grandfather. She couldn't wait for
this to end, so they could be alone and she could reassure him.

'I regret I must leave you for a short while, Miranda.'

'What?' She gazed up at him distractedly as he drew her
aside, her stomach contracting as she imagined making small
talk with his relatives. But then she saw the look in Theo's
eyes. Far from grief, his expression held all the watchfulness
and urgency she had sensed around her. 'Is something wrong?'

His lips pressed down, and he breathed as if to speak, then
thought better of it. She laid a hand on the sleeve of his
jacket, knowing she had to help him somehow. 'I understand, Theo. Don't worry about me. I'll be fine. You must
have a lot to sort out—'

'It's rather more than that,' he said, watching the ebb and
flow of relatives now they had broken into small groups.

'Politics?' Miranda guessed, murmuring discreetly, 'It's the
same in every family.'

He hummed cynically. 'While we're on the subject of families, Miranda, what did your sister think about the contract?
We haven't had a minute to talk, and it's unlikely to get any
better for quite some time.'

Miranda's faced softened into a smile as she answered
him. 'I think she approved.'

'Then will you sign?' Reaching into his breast pocket,
Theo pulled out the original copy. 'I want to make sure that,
whatever happens, your future is secure.'

'Now?'

'Better had…with so much going on it's bound to get overlooked. And I want to protect your interests.' He stared her
straight in the eyes and smiled. Then, uncapping his fountain
pen, he held it out to her.

Moving to a side table, Miranda signed the paper. Anything
to make life easier for him—and she had Emily's backing.

As she handed the contract back to him Theo exchanged glances with a group of men.

'Do you have to leave me right away?'

'Unfortunately I have a meeting to attend.'

'A meeting? Oh, no, Theo, that's not fair—'

'Don't look so worried. The staff will take care of you. They'll make sure you have everything you need.'

'I wasn't thinking of myself...' But he didn't seem to be listening. She tried again. 'Why must you be made to sit in a meeting so late at night when you are just coming to terms with the death of your grandfather? Don't these people understand anything?'

'It isn't like that, I can assure you.'

'Really?' She threw a fierce gaze around the room, encompassing all of them. 'You need time to mourn, Theo. It's an important stage in the grieving process. You should be planning the funeral, not attending a meeting—'

'I don't have time for this, Miranda. I'll find someone who will show you where to go.'

'But the formalities following a death are the foundations upon which we build the rest of our lives—'

'You have to understand that my circumstances are quite different from your own,' he said impatiently. 'Unless this family is properly managed—'

'Managed?' She stared up at him, feeling a chill run through her. Was that Theo's idea of the perfect family...one that was 'properly managed'?

'Yes, managed,' he confirmed. 'There's an awful lot of money at stake, Miranda. It changes things.'

'Does it? Can't you still have a family that cares for each other?'

As Theo sighed, Miranda could see how far apart they were on this.

'Miranda, you're a hopeless romantic.'

'Maybe so, but—'

'Understand one thing, Miranda. This isn't about grieving, or love. It's about money and power.'

When she saw how hard Theo's expression had become, Miranda felt her heart go out to him. 'Then I'm very sorry for you, Theo…for all of you.'

Before he could draw away again she put her hands around his waist and laid her head against his chest. He didn't know what to do at first, and remained stiff and unyielding. But he could hardly thrust her away in front of everyone. When she turned her head to drop a kiss on his chest, he laid his hands on her back, hoping that satisfied her requirements whilst maintaining the decorum he felt it was necessary to adopt in public.

'Oh, Theo…' Miranda smiled sadly as she lifted her face to look at him. 'Has no one given you a hug before?'

'Miranda, you're being ridiculous.' But he spoke softly, and was gentle with her as he disentangled himself. 'And now you must let me go.' He looked around until his gaze finally settled. 'Not perfect—but she'll do.'

'What are you talking about?' Miranda sighed with frustration as Theo walked away. He wasn't making it easy for her, but she wouldn't stop trying to offer him support—or behaving with the utmost self-control, she realised, when she identified the woman he was shepherding out of the shadows. 'Lexis.'

'Miranda,' Lexis said, with equal enthusiasm. 'Or should I call you Kyria Savakis now, and bow?'

'I think we both know that's not necessary.' Offering her hand, Miranda made it impossible for Lexis to refuse. 'Welcome to the Savakis—'

'Compound? Yes, I know.' Lexis cut across her, gazing around. 'And you're welcome to it.'

'Yes, well,' Theo said. 'I'll leave you two ladies to it, if you don't mind.'

'And if we do?'

He stopped. 'Sorry, Lexis, but in your case you'll just have to grit your teeth and stir your cauldron. Miranda...' Coming back to her, he cupped her face. 'I won't leave you alone a moment longer than I have to.'

Reassured, Miranda smiled as she watched Theo ushering the other men into one of the rooms off the hall.

'Touching.'

She turned at the cynical remark. 'Lexis, we are where we are, and neither of us can change a thing. But we're here for a funeral, so do you think we could call a truce?'

Lexis studied her face, and, finding her unflinching, shrugged. 'That's fine by me. So...' She looked Miranda up and down. 'You're one of them now.'

'One of them?' As Miranda followed Lexis's glance around what she had already gleaned was a materialistic gathering, she firmed her jaw. 'I can assure you, Lexis, that there is not the smallest similarity between these people and me. I'm here as Theo's wife, to support him and to offer whatever comfort I can.'

And to stand in his place as host if I have to, she added grimly to herself, following the women who were starting to file into one of the rooms off the hall. 'Will you join me, Lexis?'

'This is the small salon,' Lexis murmured discreetly, evidently mellowing enough to accompany her.

As they entered the brilliantly lit room Miranda guessed her entire family home would fit easily into the 'small' salon. 'It's very nice...'

'Nice?' Lexis raised a brow. 'And I'm sure you can't have failed to notice how friendly everyone is?'

Lexis's irony was well founded. As much as she tried to

catch anyone's attention, Miranda couldn't. It seemed everyone preferred either to sit rigidly, sipping tea, or to stand stiffly in silence, lost in thought. 'What's wrong with everyone?' she whispered to Lexis.

'This is a tense time for them.'

'What do you mean?'

'Look around the room and tell me what you see.'

'Theo's grieving relatives?' Miranda found it hard to sound convinced.

'Even *you* don't believe that,' Lexis commented cynically.

'Then explain,' Miranda pressed.

'This is a room full of women who depend for the very air they breathe on the men they married. They're all sitting here waiting for the outcome of their husbands' meeting with Theo. They want to be sure that things will remain the same now that Dimitri's dead. He always paid out to keep the relatives off his back.'

'But that's so cold-hearted of them!'

'Yes, isn't it? The only thing these women care about is that their allowances won't be hit. There's not a single person here, except for you and me, who has an interest outside the home that isn't vetted first by their husband.'

'Really? What are your interests?'

'Well, I don't sit around spending my allowance. As it happens, I run a small animal charity.'

Miranda found herself smiling at this unsuspected side to Lexis. Theo might think her a tearaway, but Lexis had more depth than he thought. 'It's not up to us to judge them, Lexis. We've been out in the world—maybe they've never had that opportunity.'

'You're too soft,' Lexis insisted. Taking Miranda's arm, she steered her towards a door that led outside. 'There is such a thing as free will, you know.'

Miranda had been wrong about Lexis, and it was a relief to find an ally in such an unexpected quarter. 'Thank goodness it will never be like that with Theo and me. I'm always going to work—'

'And he's agreed to that?'

'He can't refuse me. Music is my life—*was* my life before we met.'

'But you can't continue as a top-flight musician,' Lexis said bluntly, nodding to the attendant who was waiting to open doors for them.

'No, you're right.' Miranda was surprised to learn that it didn't hurt so much to admit it now that she had something else she felt a passion for. 'But I can carry on teaching—passing on the knowledge and experience I have gained.'

Lexis made an approving sound as they walked outside. 'Times change,' she conceded. 'At one time men like Theo were expected to marry virgins and make a dynastic match. And a dynastic match is still expected in families like ours. Take me, for instance.' Linking arms with Miranda, Lexis drew her further into the garden. 'My father wanted me to marry Theo.'

'And did you want to?'

'That's not the point, Miranda. Whether I wanted to or not, I was sent over to Kalmos for Theo's inspection like a prize heifer.'

'But that's outrageous!'

'No, Miranda, that's business. Fortunately Theo didn't buy into the idea, and had enough sense to ship me home.'

'But why did you go along with it?'

'I love my father…'

A look of understanding passed between them.

'At least if Theo lets you work you'll always retain your independence.'

'There's no if about it.' Miranda smiled at Lexis. 'I have no intention of ever becoming completely dependent on a man. I almost went down that route once—emotionally, at least—believing my confidence to perform was based solely on the approval of my teacher or my manager, when in actual fact it was up to me to put in the work and make sure I was good enough to stand before an audience. I think it's important never to lose sight of your own identity, however much you love someone.'

'You really mean that, don't you?'

Instead of sharing her mood of optimism, Lexis's face had clouded over. 'Yes, of course I do,' Miranda said, wondering why Lexis had suddenly grown so quiet. 'Were you in love with Theo?' she asked gently.

'What if I was? He never wanted me. It was just a cold-blooded business deal cooked up by my father and Dimitri Savakis to merge two great shipping lines. I could have told my father that a man like Theo would never go along with it, but he wouldn't listen.'

'I'm really sorry.'

'Don't be. I can look after myself.'

As Lexis tipped her chin, Miranda smiled. 'Well, if you ever need a friend…'

'I appreciate that. And I'm sorry too, because I thought you were like all the rest, looking for a meal ticket, and now I know you're not.'

Miranda wondered why Lexis seemed so uneasy. 'Is there something else? Something you're not telling me?'

Lexis looked at her, and then her gaze faltered, as if she was trying to find the words to voice some unpalatable truth.

'Come on—tell me what's worrying you,' Miranda pressed. 'Surely we can trust each other now?'

Lexis sighed and firmed her lips.

'Is it about Theo? If you think he will make it difficult for me to be independent now we're married, you're wrong, Lexis. I'm going to create scholarships for promising music students, and Theo has agreed to help me with the administration—'

'You really don't have any idea why Theo married you, do you?'

'He loves me…' Miranda's brave statement tailed away as she saw the expression in Lexis's eyes. 'Lexis?' she prompted.

'I'm so sorry. You don't deserve this.'

Miranda steeled herself. 'Go on.'

'Theo had to marry because Dimitri made it a condition of his will.'

'Dimitri's will? What are you talking about? No.' Miranda shook her head. She was definite on this point. 'Theo married me because he loves me and because of all this—' She gestured back towards the room where all Theo's dependents were waiting with their stony faces. 'Theo wants a loving family, and I can give him that.'

Lexis made a sound of frustration. 'Theo hasn't got a romantic bone in his body. I don't know what he told you, but this was never some idyllic "love at first sight" nonsense for him. Theo planned this marriage cold-bloodedly for no better reason than to gain power and control over the Savakis shipping line.'

'Power and control?' Miranda gave an incredulous laugh. 'I can put your mind at rest there. My family has no influence in the circles in which Theo moves—even if my twin did marry a prince.' Her conviction was growing stronger—Lexis had made a terrible mistake.

'You still don't get it, do you?'

'I think you'd better tell me everything you know,' Miranda pressed. She had done enough running away to know that unpleasantness only followed you around. This time she was going to face up to whatever Lexis had to say, and then decide what to do.

'All right,' Lexis began hesitantly. 'Dimitri made it a condition of his will that Theo must be married if he was to inherit the controlling interest in the Savakis shipping company—otherwise he'd lose the lot. Dimitri wanted to be sure that the dynastic line would continue.'

Miranda said nothing for a while, and then, raising her head, she stared Lexis in the eyes. 'So I'm the prize heifer?'

'I'm really sorry, Miranda, but I'm betting no one else would have told you.'

The meeting had ended, and the goal he had aimed for had been reached. Now it was on to the next challenge, Theo reflected, smiling to himself as he gathered up all the papers in front of him.

His mind was uncharacteristically packed with romantic thoughts. Miranda touched him in a way no one had before. The sound of her voice was enough to fill him with love. She was so tender, so devoted, and though he had tried to harden his heart and concentrate solely on business, on this day of all days, she had brought his whole life into clear focus with something as simple as a hug, had shown him what really mattered.

He'd spent his life pushing people away, knowing most had been paid to make a fuss of him. It had bred a coldness in him. He hadn't known how to be affectionate until Miranda. But she had shown him how to love without restraint, without boundaries, proving just as she'd done before the meeting that a simple touch or a tender glance was worth more than all the power and money in the world.

He was greedy for more, and he wanted to show her the same devotion. He wanted to prove how special she was and forge a future for them both, a future his grandfather had been denied. It might be too late to make his peace with the old man, but with Miranda at his side he could found the dynasty that had meant so much to Dimitri.

It hadn't been easy for her since they met, and circumstances had turned their honeymoon on its head, but still she was taking everything in her stride. He would make it up to her. He could concentrate on being a good husband now that the contract was signed and his position as chairman of the board had been confirmed.

'No, thank you, gentlemen,' he said as someone offered him a second glass of champagne. 'If you will excuse me, I'm going to celebrate with my wife.'

CHAPTER TWELVE

'MIRANDA. At last! I didn't think I was ever going to get away. Thank goodness someone showed you to our room. Is it all right for you? We can move if you don't like it…'

Even as he hunkered down beside the sofa to take her hand Theo realised something vital had changed between them. 'Miranda?' Ice sluiced through his veins as she turned to stare at him.

'Is it true, Theo?'

'Is what true?' He couldn't pretend he didn't know. Miranda's face was like an open book to him, and right now all the pages were twisted with hurt and disbelief.

'Did you marry me in order to secure your grasp on the Savakis shipping line?'

'Who told you that?'

'It doesn't matter who told me. Is it true?'

'Miranda… Come and sit with me for a moment. Let me explain—'

'*Explain?*'

He blenched and turned away. With that single word she had managed to express all the disillusionment he had heaped upon her.

'How can you explain that I was just part of your business strategy, Theo? And why can't you look at me if it isn't true?'

He had been so buoyed up as he raced to their room, so exhilarated by the plans spinning round his head. What could he possibly say to reassure her now that it wasn't a lie?

He couldn't lie to her.

'Everything you say is true, Miranda. I didn't start out on this with the best of motives—'

'*This?*' She interrupted him. 'This marriage, do you mean?'

'Don't make this any harder than it has to be.'

'How much harder does it get, Theo?'

Her voice was breaking, and it cut right through him. But what frightened him most was the way she was looking at him with such furious disdain.

'You said you would never hurt me. You said we were marrying quickly because you couldn't wait to make me your bride. You said you wanted to share Kalmos, your favourite place on earth with me—remember that, Theo?'

'Miranda, please…'

'Get off me, Theo!' she warned him in a furious cold voice. 'You manipulated me. You made me sign a contract when I didn't realise what it entailed. You deceived me, and you deceived my sister—'

'I put every safeguard on earth in place for you—'

'You bought me like a whore!'

'Don't say that!'

'You bought me with tarnished coin—'

'I gave you money to make you feel secure!'

'Do you really think you can buy anything, Theo? Even a wife?'

'That's not what I intended.'

'Well, goodness knows what you *did* intend!'

'Your happiness and security mean everything to me—'

'My happiness? My security? You said you loved me, Theo, and I believed you. In the light of what I know now, your love doesn't count for anything.'

'Nevertheless, I do love you,' he said simply.

With a contemptuous exclamation Miranda sprang to her feet. 'Well, if this is your idea of love, you can keep it! And you can keep this, too.' Tugging off her wedding ring, she flung it at him. It rolled across the marble floor and skittered to a halt at his feet.

'What can I say to make you believe me?'

'Nothing.'

'I left the meeting to be with you. You're all that matters to me. You're the most important thing in the world to me—'

'Is that right?'

'When did you become so cold, Miranda?'

She gave a short, humourless laugh. 'Strangely enough, not when I learned that you had married me to acquire the controlling interest in the Savakis shipping line, but later—when I had read this.' She slapped her hand onto a document on the table. 'Dimitri's will. That was when I realised that you had only tied me into our marriage for sixty days because Dimitri's will stipulated that we must remain together for thirty days before the share transfer could take place. You really wanted to make sure of me, didn't you, Theo?'

He tensed. 'How did you get a copy of Dimitri's will?'

'It's surprising how accommodating people become when you bear the Savakis name. I have discovered that I only have to ask and I receive.'

'What are you talking about?'

'I went into the hub of Dimitri's world—his office,' she clarified, when Theo looked puzzled. 'Wasn't it you who said that the business meant everything to your grandfather? So I really wasn't surprised to discover that he kept a full secretarial service here, or that they were working overtime tonight. It was a small matter to say that you had sent me for a copy of your grandfather's will,' she continued mercilessly. 'They were hardly going to refuse me—hardly going to express surprise that you had sent me, a mere woman, to run an errand for you.'

'Miranda…' Theo wiped a hand across his face as if he couldn't bear to see what she had discovered reflected in her eyes.

'No wonder you faxed only that handwritten contract to my sister. If you had sent Emily a copy of your grandfather's will I suspect her response would have been very different.'

'And you've read the will?'

'Of course. There's no need for me to spell it out for you, is there, Theo?'

Dipping down, he picked up her wedding ring and, balancing it on the flat of his hand, held it out to her. 'I'd like to tell you that you're mistaken, Miranda, but I can't. Our marriage has to last for thirty days before the share transfer can be completed. Tonight I was voted unanimously onto the Savakis board as chairman, but that means nothing in practical terms without a controlling interest in the business. It would make me the puppet of greedy, unscrupulous men and I would have to resign. If I had done this…' he closed his hand around her wedding ring '…for my sake alone, then, yes, I would be as guilty as you paint me. But the future of too many people is hanging in the balance, and I have to think of them.'

'And for this you were prepared to sacrifice not only your own happiness but that of whichever woman was unfortunate enough to come along at the right moment?'

'Yes,' he admitted bluntly.

Touching her hand to her head, Miranda made a sound of incredulity. Closing her eyes, she shut him out.

'I realise that this has been a less than perfect start to our marriage—'

'*What?*' She cut across him with disbelief. 'This isn't the start of anything, Theo. There is no marriage.'

'Please put this on again, Miranda.'

'You are joking?' She stared at the ring he was holding out to her.

'No, I'm perfectly serious. Like I said, too many people are depending on me to get this right for it to stop now.'

'And what about me, Theo?'

The resolve in his face only intensified. 'Stop thinking about yourself, and help me help them.'

'I'm not frightened of sacrifice, Theo, but I do like to know what's expected of me from the start.'

'I've never asked you to do anything you don't want to do—have I, Miranda?'

'Do you know what you're asking?'

'For you to act as if everything's all right—for you to support me for the next thirty days. I'm asking for your help, Miranda.'

She was in turmoil. Before she had opened her eyes and seen the truth behind their marriage she would have laid down her life for him. 'But I love you…and you lied to me.'

'I loved you from the first moment we met.'

'You swore at me and called me an idiot!'

'We Greeks are a passionate people,' he murmured. 'However I felt at the precise moment we met, I love you here and now. We've here for the funeral of my grandfather Dimitri,' he continued, reining in his passion. 'Is it too much to expect my wife to stand at my side?'

'The same wife who played such a crucial if unwitting role in your victory at the board meeting today, Theo?'

'It's late.' He ignored her jibe as he glanced at his wristwatch. 'And I still have many people to see. You can stay here in the room, and I will arrange for the helicopter to take you back to the yacht, where you can collect your things and return home, or you can come downstairs with me and play your part. It's up to you, Miranda.'

'Can't these people wait until tomorrow?'

Theo gave her a look that suggested she had a lot to learn about her new relatives. 'Most of them will leave the moment the funeral is over. I imagine those who have already spoken to me and received their cheques will be packing now.'

Miranda exhaled slowly, trying to comprehend the new world in which she found herself. 'And what about the people who worked for your grandfather?'

'What about them?'

'I thought we had come here to offer comfort?'

'Comfort?' He lost patience with her. 'I'm here to write cheques.'

'But surely *some* of the staff must have cared for your grandfather?'

'Cared for him?' Walking across to pick up a decanter, he poured himself a drink. 'Do you mean like that group of vultures waiting downstairs?'

'No, Theo, I'm thinking of Dimitri's valet, his butler...I don't know.' The number of staff who might work in a house as large as this one was beyond her ken. 'There must be people in this house who have been affected by your grandfather's death. Don't you think we should find out who they are and try to help them?'

'We?' He swallowed his drink in a single gulp and swung around.

'People must be worried about their jobs, Theo. They need reassurance.'

She was right, he realised, but what was she saying? 'I

thought, like the rest of them, you couldn't wait to get away from me?' He made an impatient gesture. 'Well, here's your chance, Miranda. I'll deal with them.'

'We'll deal with them together,' she said coolly.

He still had her wedding ring clenched tight in his fist. She had made no move to take it back, and that riled him. But did he want to be married to some compliant milksop? 'Haven't you forgotten something?'

'Have I?'

Holding out the ring, he held her stare.

She didn't move. 'And your grandfather's staff?'

'All right! I'll call for Dimitri's major-domo and see if he can help us.'

They had worked their way steadily through the queue of relatives, and Theo was forced to concede that it would have been a lot harder without Miranda at his side. She was good at finding the right words—while he wrote the cheques.

He had issued a warning to all the idlers. They would have to fund their extravagant lifestyles themselves from now on, or draw in their horns—because he had something better to spend his money on. He had taken pleasure in outlining Miranda's plans to them, pretending not to see how her cheeks flushed red at every mention of it.

'We can't stop now,' she said, the moment he put his pen away.

He stood and stretched. 'It's getting late.'

'Nevertheless, we still have people to see…'

As he turned and met her gaze he felt a spear of longing and regret. He heard an echo from the past, the voice of his own mother, who had fought a losing battle against the idleness and excesses of his father. Was he in danger of turning into Acteon Savakis? The thought appalled him. But the thought that Miranda might have the same steel in her back-bone as his mother had the opposite effect.

They sat up late, meeting every member of the household staff as Miranda had insisted. Theo explained that, in the Savakis way, Dimitri's funeral would be held the following morning. Everyone had their own lives to get back to, he said. And he was right about his relatives: the moment they had pocketed their cheques all their talk was of travel plans.

They were drinking coffee when Theo told her that their wedding blessing would have to be postponed.

'We have a few things to iron out before we talk about blessings.' Miranda stared at him steadily. Theo held her gaze, as if measuring her resolve.

'Well, I'm tired,' he said, 'and we'll only have a few hours' sleep as it is. So we'll talk about it after breakfast—'

'No, Theo.' She tensed inside. He made it all sound so cosy and predictable, so neatly ordered to suit his will. 'I can't just forget everything that's happened.'

She saw his face change and knew that he had imagined she was over her tantrum. For in Theo's eyes that was all it was. Her manner had been calm and relaxed as they had talked to people, and that had reassured him. He seemed to think he could brush everything under the table and start again.

'I'd like to eat breakfast privately—just you and me,' she said. 'It will give us a chance to discuss where we go from here—'

'Where we go from here?' He cut across her. 'I would have thought that was obvious—back to the yacht. And as for dining alone? Like so many of your ideas, Miranda, romantic, but impracticable. We must breakfast with everyone else. It is important that I provide strong leadership. The Savakis clan must be one unified force. I can't afford to have the family splitting into factions because they think I'm ruled by my wife.'

'Don't try and simplify everything, Theo, by blithely telling me that we're going back to your yacht. You know what I'm talking about. What's happened between us is far too serious to dismiss. And as for being ruled by your wife—surely you are ruled by your loss, and by your wish to receive comfort from your wife?'

'So you have comfort to spare for me?' He gazed at her cynically.

'Yes, Theo. In spite of the fact that you have treated me shabbily, I do know what a strain this must have been for you.'

A strain? His lips curved in an ironic line. This was the norm for him—this battle to remain at the top of a greasy pole. As far as his feelings for Dimitri were concerned, it was too late for him to pretend there had been any real connection between them other than blood and business. He regretted that now. He regretted the fact that they had both let pride get in the way of what might have been.

'I don't want to be unreasonable,' Miranda said, reclaiming his attention, 'or make things harder for you. So I suggest we have breakfast with your relatives, attend the service and host the wake, and then meet afterwards in private.'

'You're calling a meeting?' He wanted to smile, but wisely suppressed the urge.

'Yes—unless you're too busy to see me?'

He ignored the sarcasm. 'That's not an unreasonable request.'

His business skills had always outstripped his people skills, and he wondered about the strain on Miranda. She had been involved in an accident that had stolen so much from her—not just her career, but a family who adored her. And now this… He should reassure her. Hell, he wanted her back.

'When we have the blessing—'

'*If*, Theo.'

He pressed on. 'I want you to tell your family everything you've told me about the accident. I want you to tell them about the prognosis on your hand, and the fact that we're going to try again with another doctor, and I want you to tell them about your idea for the scholarship scheme. I want you to tell them everything, Miranda, and I want you to promise me now that you will.'

Her eyes filled with tears. 'So many promises, Theo. How many of them do we keep?'

She was drawn tight like a bowstring, and the last thing he wanted now was to provoke another outburst of emotion. They were both exhausted, and if anything was to be salvaged from their relationship they needed peace above everything else.

'You're tired. It's been a long night.'

'I'll tell my family in my own time,' she said firmly.

She was more resilient than he'd ever given her credit for, but that same strength could take her away from him. He couldn't let that happen yet—for the sake of the business as well as for himself. But she meant so much to him that once the conditions of Dimitri's will were met if only leaving him would make her happy, then he would let her go.

But if she did go, then he had to be sure the rift with her family was properly healed. 'By keeping the details of the accident to yourself you have turned your face from people who love you, people who want to help and support you—'

'People like you, do you mean?'

'I was thinking of your family.'

'I have never wanted to be a burden to them.'

'A burden? Don't they love you?'

'Of course they do—'

'And yet you deny them the right to show their love for you?'

'How I handle things is up to me, Theo. At least I have experienced a warm and loving family.'

He frowned at her use of the past tense. 'Meaning what?'

'Meaning that for all your money and power, and your proud boast of a Savakis clan, at present all you head is a collection of dysfunctional money-grubbing wasters.'

He almost laughed out loud as he stood up. Did she think he didn't know that? But somehow it thrilled him to hear her say it—to know she'd got the measure of them so quickly. 'I'll see you at breakfast, Miranda. I'm sure you'll be relieved to hear that I've had my things moved to an adjoining suite of rooms for our remaining time here.'

Miranda wasn't relieved. In fact she had never felt so lonely, so cold, or so uncertain about the future. She had vowed to seize control of her life, and now it was running away with her again.

She supposed she should be grateful she had been spared the nightmare. Instead of thrashing about in the grip of some dreadful dream, she had spent the night staring at the ornate cobwebby drapes hanging in her room, wondering what wildlife they might harbour. The high bed had a lumpy mattress, and the only good thing was that dawn came quickly. She noticed the first pale strands of light while she was raining blows down on the pillows.

The early part of the day passed in a blur of duty, with the sticking plaster of formality to hold it all together. Once the funeral was over there was a mad scramble to see who could be first to leave the Savakis stronghold.

She found Theo waiting for her in the hall with his overnight bag at his side.

'What about our meeting?'

'Nothing's changed.'

'But you're ready to leave,' she said, puzzled.

'Ah, here's your case now.'

Miranda turned to see one of the servants carrying it down

the stairs. 'What? You promised me that we'd have a meeting today once everything had quietened down—'

'And so we will—but on the yacht.'

'That's not what I agreed.'

'You didn't specify a venue,' he pointed out.

'Very clever, Theo.'

'It's time to leave—unless you want to stay here?'

How stealthily he had manipulated the situation—patiently, confidently baiting the trap. Theo was a consummate predator, Miranda realised. There were no fanfares, no crass displays of strength—no wonder he was so successful in business. He moved in like a black panther, his looks and easy manner distracting from his main purpose which was always the same: to win, to defeat, to prevail.

'You know I don't want to stay here,' she said tensely.

'Then shall we go?'

'Do we have to keep the electric fences?' Miranda murmured as Theo's helicopter soared high above the compound. She was thinking aloud, weighing the grain of an idea against a whole silo full of reasons why she should leave him.

'My grandfather had many enemies. I am not so controversial a figure.'

'So are you saying they don't have to stay?'

'Why are you asking?'

'Oh, no reason. I just can't imagine what you will do with such a place. You surely don't intend to live there?'

'No, I hope to renovate my late parents' home on Kalmos. This island is more convenient for the mainland and the airport, thanks to the bridge, but I don't think anyone could make a home out of the Savakis compound, do you?'

As Theo turned to look at her Miranda knew she had to

make a decision. 'A home, no. But it would make an impressive music *conservatoire*.'

Theo's expression was hidden from her behind a sweep of black lashes, but her gaze was drawn to his mouth and to the faint smile playing around his lips.

'We'll discuss it another time,' he said, turning away from her to gaze out of the cockpit.

Their arrival back on the yacht was so smooth, so effortless, that within a few short hours they had slipped back into shipboard life as if they had never been away.

But Miranda started packing immediately. She drew the line at sharing a bed with Theo. He took everything for granted. He was so certain he had everything under his control. But she couldn't forget that he had lied to her. He had tricked her into marrying him quite simply to ensure his grip on the Savakis shipping line, and he hadn't made any attempt to explain or apologise. Instead he thought he could buy her compliance, with his promise to support her scholarship proposal.

She still wanted him. She had seen a dream and had believed it could come true. But how could she ever forgive what he had done? Theo was acting as if nothing unusual had happened between them. His clothes and possessions were still in their stateroom, a clear signal that he thought she would be happy to forgive and forget now they were safely back on his territory.

He didn't knock before coming in. Of course he didn't knock, Miranda realised tensely, turning to see Theo standing behind her.

'I thought we might take a walk on deck?'

He looked past her towards the bed, where her suitcase lay open, as he spoke, and instinctively she moved in front of it, shielding it from his gaze.

'What are you doing?'

His voice was soft, but it chilled her. 'What does it look like?' She held his gaze, determined he wouldn't change her mind.

'Don't be facetious with me, Miranda. I asked you a question. Why are you packing your suitcase?'

'Because when we dock I'm leaving you, Theo.'

'Leaving me? You can't do that.'

'I think you'll find that I can.' *And I will*, she vowed silently. She had weighed her dream against a future of compliance and found it lacking in every essential. Without freedom, without spirit, without self-determination, she would have nothing to offer her students.

Theo moved so fast he had hold of her arms before she realised he had crossed the room. 'I won't let you do this! Are you listening to me, Miranda?' he demanded when she turned her face.

'No!' With an angry jerk she broke free. 'I've finished with listening to you, Theo. I've done my duty as you asked. I stood by your side at Dimitri's funeral, and supported you in every way I can—'

'Except when it comes to breaking the contract you signed?'

'Is that all you can think about?' Feelings welled in her throat when he didn't answer. 'Unlike you, Theo, I do have some finer feelings, and though I don't want to be used by you, I don't want to cause distress to your co-workers either. I'll stay married to you for thirty days, so that you can benefit from the share transfer, but there's nothing in the contract to say I have to live with you during that time.'

'I thought we were going to discuss this first?'

'Is this your idea of a discussion?' She opened her arms wide and he took a step back.

'You called the meeting, so talk.'

'A meeting which you chose to reschedule without consulting me. Good grief, Theo! Just listen to us! Call this a marriage? You wouldn't know how to conduct a personal relationship with a puppy, let alone with a wife.' Picking up a dress she started folding it, needing something, anything, to keep her from breaking down.

'Perhaps it's not too late for me to learn…'

She didn't soften. 'The first thing you have to learn is not to use all those subtle, scheming manipulative tactics you use in business, Theo. Surprisingly, people you are trying to engage in a relationship don't take too well to being duped.'

'There's only one person I'm interested in engaging in a relationship with—'

'You lied to me, Theo. You lied and tricked me into marriage.' Miranda allowed the clothes she was folding to drop from her hands. 'And you've said nothing to reassure me since we returned. And what was it all for, Theo? More money, more power, and a hideous mausoleum?'

'You agreed to marry me. I didn't force you.' Theo took another step back, feeling an inferno rising inside him. Miranda provoked feelings that went so deep and were so fundamental it frightened him. He felt as if he was about to embark on the fight of his life. 'And I suppose you have nothing to gain from this marriage? Have you forgotten your music students so easily?

'I had hoped to gain a husband who was a man of his word!'

'Are you calling me a liar, Miranda?' His pride would take many blows, but not that one. 'And where do you think you will go when you leave me?' he pressed, when she dug her hands into the suitcase and carried on packing. 'Back home for some more humiliation? To spend the rest of your life wallowing in self-pity?'

'How dare you say that?'

Her voice was like a whiplash and her eyes were emerald ice. Her face was ashen, except for two red blotches on her cheeks, and every part of her was tense. Her lips were white, and her poor damaged hand was balled into a fist by her side. But at least he had provoked a reaction. He pushed some more. 'Are you going to keep running all your life, Miranda? Or just this once are you going to find the guts to stay and fight?'

The cruel words hurt him a lot more than they hurt her— and they hurt her a lot. He waited tensely, watching her expression change from shock, to anger, and then again to the awakening of another possibility—that just this one time he might be right.

'What if I've no fight left in me?'

It was as if she was asking herself the question.

'I don't believe that for a moment.'

'You won't change my mind, Theo.' Refocusing, she gazed at him. 'I've made my decision. I'm going home to my parents.'

'So, you *are* running away?'

'No...' Slamming the case shut, she rounded on him. 'I've stopped running. I thought that would have been obvious, since I'm going back, not running away.'

'Back home, where you think life will be easier?'

'I don't expect anything to be easy.'

'Well, that's something—because take it from an expert, life is never easy, and if you turn your back on problems they just grow.'

'I'm only turning my back on you, Theo. Nothing else.'

'Well, that makes a change.'

She stared at him. 'What did you say?'

'Are you going to see another doctor about your hand?'

'Yes! No... Well, not right away.'

He cocked his head and viewed her sceptically. 'So nothing changes?'

'I didn't say that.'

'You didn't have to. I think you're just scared, Miranda. Scared of facing up to what the future might hold. Instead of exploring every avenue, you prefer to hide your head in the sand and pretend the accident never happened.'

'And if I stay with you all that will change?'

Her voice was strained, verging on hysteria. It frightened him. It told him that whatever she was hiding was so bad it could take her from him. 'Yes,' he said fiercely. 'If you stay with me I will make you face the truth. There have been too many secrets between us already, and if we're to make a success of this marriage we have to be completely open with each other…and honest to ourselves.'

'You *dare* to lecture me on the benefits of truth?'

'I dare to change. Do you, Miranda?'

'You talk as if I can just put all this behind me and start again. You talk about our marriage as if it had been built on sound foundations and a little more mortar is all that is needed to put it to rights—'

'Is there a sounder foundation than love?'

'Love built on lies?'

'You can't leave me. I won't let you,' he said flatly.

'I think you'll find that the law in my country allows a woman to change her mind if she discovers that her marriage was a mistake.'

'And is that what our marriage has become, Miranda— a mistake?'

'It always was a mistake, only I didn't realise it. I loved you, Theo, loved you completely. And, yes, love was blind. I walked into this with my eyes wide open, but I didn't see a thing. And now I'm walking out again.'

'Don't forget you signed a contract—'

'The terms of which, as I have already told you, I have no intention of breaking.'

'What if I refuse to let you go?' He moved menacingly, one step towards the door.

'I don't think you'd want to keep me here against my will, Theo.'

'Try me.'

As Theo stared at her, Miranda was surprised to feel her breathing quicken. The curve of his lips, the set of his jaw, the look in his eyes… She was being bombarded by so many conflicting messages, each of them guaranteed to set her heart-rate soaring. Heated emotions between a man and woman could lead to dangerous consequences. Anyone knew that. And now there was danger all around her, and she was causing most of it.

CHAPTER THIRTEEN

How could Theo do this to her? How could he make her want him so badly when all this was happening—and with nothing more than a look?

Reason had no part to play. There was a dragging sensation all the way from the pulse beating hectically in her neck to the apex of her thighs...

'Miranda?'

Swallowing hard, she muttered something indistinct.

'Shouldn't you be packing?'

There was too much innuendo in his voice. Arousal was surging through her so that when she tried to nod her head she shook it instead.

'Well, then?'

Theo's firm tone, the unyielding stance, everything that had drawn her to him in the first place...

She didn't want this—this oblivion, this chance to escape. She wanted to run as far and as fast as she could from him, to try and forget what she felt for him, as well as what she had lost. But given a choice to rail at Theo and have his cold face turned against her, or to lose herself in a world where the only reality was sensation—

'Have you decided what you want yet, Miranda?'

As Theo eased onto one hip and stared at her with his dark, lazy gaze, she knew he was utterly confident of her response. He knew he had awakened an undreamed-of hunger in her, and that now that hunger was demanding to be fed.

'Or do you need me to tell you what to do this time?'

Beneath the prim white shirt her heart was thundering. Theo had made no attempt to come any closer, but it was as if there was an invisible rope, drawing her in. She resisted it, physically holding herself back.

He moved away from the door, as if to show her that she could go if she wanted to. She exhaled a ragged sigh of relief—of regret. But then, turning swiftly, he locked the door and went to lean back against the wall.

'You know you want to,' he murmured.

One last time? She did—and so very badly. Taking her time, she walked across the room and stood in front of him.

'It might be easier if you slip off your briefs first.'

'You mean here—against the wall?' It was so cold-blooded, as though Theo was performing an exercise in self-control.

Miranda searched for some strength to resist him, but found herself staring at his lips instead, and then on into a gaze full of irony and self-assurance. She started as he traced the outline of her body with his fingertips. Was it possible anyone could deny they wanted this? And then her thoughts shattered into infinite shards of lust as he turned her and pressed her back against the wall.

'Are you going to take them off, or shall I?' he murmured, freeing the buttons on his fly.

As his fingers slipped beneath the waistband of her briefs, Miranda's gaze was drawn to the jutting erection so clearly defined beneath his casual chinos.

'Quickly,' he murmured, and he only had to brush his lips

against her neck to make her gasp. 'Good girl. Now, spread your legs and bend your knees…a little more…perfect.'

He couldn't allow her to leave him. In business when every door had been slammed in his face he'd always found a window. He never gave up. He had a dream, and Miranda had given him that dream; he wasn't about to let her take it back.

Testing her readiness, he took her firmly, without delay, driving home to the hilt. 'Is this what you want, Miranda? Is this what you need?' He heard her whimper of agreement, felt her trembling as he withdrew to thrust again. And this time he supported her, cupping her buttocks to lift her off the ground. 'Do you want more, Miranda? Yes? Then let me hear you say it…'

She gasped out her answer, and for a few moments he obliged, but then, releasing his grip carefully, making sure she didn't sink to the floor, he withdrew completely.

'Theo?' she managed at last, panting.

'So will you stay with me?'

'You—'

'Fiend?' He supplied confidently.

'You'll stop at nothing, will you?'

'That's right.' And there were more pleasurable ways of achieving his goal than she would ever know. Unless she stayed. 'So should I stop now?'

'Don't you dare.'

Dragging her into his arms, he kissed her deeply, and as she moulded against him he swept her up and carried her to the bed. Stripping off the rest of her clothes, he took off his own with her help, and then, taking her into his arms he gave her everything, bringing her beneath him and plunging deep.

Holding her firmly, he brought her maximum pleasure, maximum excitement, with every stroke driving the message home. She needed him every bit as much as he needed her.

For different reasons, maybe, but there was no escape for either of them. When the lines of destiny crossed, as theirs had done, there could be no turning back.

The abandoned suitcase was a potent symbol. It gave him a rush just to see it lying there, Theo realised as he walked back into the stateroom from the bathroom, where he had been showering. The maids would hang up her things again.

Swinging a towel around his neck, to catch the drips from his hair, he gazed at his wife's sleeping form. Miranda's limbs were spread across three-quarters of the mattress in a pose that was both innocent and provocative.

It was generally accepted that a woman's primary drive was the desire to build a nest and have a family, while a man was driven by the need to mate. But in his marriage that hypothesis had been turned on its head. The events of the past few days had crystallised his thoughts and proved to him that what he wanted more than anything in the world was not the power and wealth Miranda seemed to think he craved, but a family. Simply that… Except nothing was ever that simple. He had to win her trust again. It wasn't enough to hold her with sex; he wanted more, a lot more, from the mother of his children.

'Miranda? Miranda, wake up.' He needed to see her face, to look into her eyes, see what they might hold for him. Snatching up his robe from the chair where he had discarded it, he tugged it on, belting it firmly.

'Theo, what is it?'

She reached out to him sleepily, her eyes still closed, her voice soft and beguiling. He wanted nothing more than to go back to bed and make love to her. 'Wake up, *agape mou*. I have to talk to you.'

'Our meeting?' she breathed, stretching provocatively. 'Can't that wait, Theo?'

It was too much temptation, but he resisted. 'No, this can't wait, Miranda. I need to speak to you now.'

Hearing the change in his voice, she sat up, brushing her hair from her face. 'Theo, what is it? What's wrong?'

'I want you to get up so that we can talk. It's important. Shower, dress, and I'll call for some food. We'll eat here, on the veranda outside.'

'I'd like that.' She rubbed her eyes.

He didn't think she sounded so certain—and who could blame her? Lovemaking was uppermost in his mind too. He ached to be deep inside her again, but they could spend their whole life having sex and nothing would change.

She came back quickly, dressed in a towelling robe with her hair still wet and hanging down her back in a sleek inky curtain.

'You're dripping,' he murmured, lifting the towel from her shoulders to mop her face.

'Then dry me,' she suggested, letting the robe fall open.

'Later,' he promised, retrieving the belt and securing it.

Drawing her out onto the balcony, he sat next to her on the sofa and drew her close. Then, taking her hand, he removed the wedding band.

'What are you doing?' she said, stiffening.

'It's good between us, Miranda…in bed.'

What was he going to say next, this man who had taught her to trust again and then betrayed her? The man she loved more than life itself…the man she knew, for all her bravado, she couldn't bear to lose.

Seeing her wedding band glittering on Theo's open palm made Miranda feel as if Theo had reached into her chest, taken hold of her heart and twisted it.

He was right: it *was* good between them in bed. Theo had taken her to the extremes of sexual love and brought her back again safely in a way she had thought would never be possible. Was he saying that was all there could ever be between them? And should she want any more when she was tied to this marriage by a contract she had been tricked into signing?

'I want more than sex in my marriage.'

He sounded detached, but utterly determined. It made a shiver course down her spine. Was this the end? And, if it was, shouldn't she be relieved that his betrayal had reached its inevitable conclusion?

'I want love.' Theo spoke softly, almost as if voicing his thoughts, and then, chewing down on his lip, he slipped her a wry smile. 'You see, Miranda, sex isn't enough for me.'

Love? He wanted love?

His wry humour didn't surprise her. Theo used humour as a shield in the same way she used anger about the accident to fuel her fear of coming under anyone's influence again. But could she lay aside her insecurities? Staring at him, she found she couldn't look away. Did she need love so badly she was prepared to give their marriage another try?

'It's been a tortuous process getting this far,' he admitted, 'and I guess we could both walk away—'

'Is that what you want, Theo?'

'You have to trust me before we can move on.'

'How can I do that? You don't know how far I've come in how short a time. And that was all because of you, because I trusted you. But now…now I don't know what to think.'

'I'm sorry I hurt you. I did what I had to do—'

'Regardless of the consequences?'

'The consequence is that we are married. The question now is do we stay married?'

'You talk so sensibly, so unemotionally, Theo, I could almost believe you when you say you want more from a marriage than sex. But love? You talk of love when I don't think you have the remotest idea what it means to love someone.'

'So you would walk away on the basis that I don't express myself as well as you do?'

'I'd stay if I thought I could trust you never to betray me again.'

'Must I prove myself to you over and over again, Miranda? When will it stop? When will you be satisfied?' He looked wounded. 'I've explained my reasons, and I'm a proud man— I'm tired of playing games. You have rights in this marriage, with or without a contract, but please remember that I have rights too.'

'You forfeited your rights with your pride, Theo, and your blind acceptance of the Savakis family rulebook that allows for no mercy, no understanding, no flexibility. You have lived your life by those rules, and they have brought you great success in the world of business, but because of them you talk of love as if it can be written into a contract like anything else. Well, it can't. And I don't recognise your rulebook.'

'And you accuse *me* of pride? Listen to yourself, Miranda.'

Lifting her hands, she let them drop back to her sides. 'If only *you* would listen to me, Theo, perhaps then you'd understand that for everything that's been missing in your life I had love to plug the gap. But you took that love and, not recognising it for what it was, you squandered it. If only you'd been honest with me from the start—'

'You would have accepted my proposal?' he asked dryly. It was the first flicker of doubt he'd seen in her eyes. 'No, I didn't think so.'

Silence fell between them.

'So is fate the enemy?' he said at last.

'What do you mean?'

'Well, by your own admission we should never have met,

and we should certainly never have married, and yet here we are. I'd call that fate, wouldn't you?'

'We're here because you needed a wife and because, foolishly, I allowed myself to fall in love with you.'

'I don't think we have any control over love. I don't think we can decide not to fall in love with someone. I think we just do—as I fell in love with you. Not because it was convenient, or because I felt sorry for you, but because I couldn't help myself.'

'What are you saying?' Miranda stared at him. Theo was speaking in the considered manner he always adopted when he had something important to say, but the words and the expression in his eyes told her that this time it was different.

'I'm saying that I love you. I'm saying that I want to spend a lot longer than sixty days with you. I'm saying that I want to spend the rest of my life with you. I'm asking you if you will wear my ring.' As he spoke, he slipped down onto one knee on the ground in front of her. 'Will you be my wife, Miranda?'

'Will you be my husband?'

She asked him in a way that left him in no doubt as to what his priorities would have to be if he wanted to keep her. 'I will,' he vowed.

They never got round to eating breakfast. Miranda barely waited until the steward had left them before getting up to lock the door. The diamonds in the wedding band Theo had replaced on her finger glittered in the sunlight as she returned to the veranda, but before she could join him Theo got up from the sofa and, pausing in the entrance, held her gaze.

Taking hold of the lapels of his robe, she drew him close. Lacing her fingers into his hair, she pulled him down to her and kissed him deeply. Capturing her face in his hands, Theo deepened the kiss until she moved against him, wanting more.

'You've learned no patience,' he chastised her softly.

'You've taught me none.'

''Then I must remedy the situation...' Resting his hands on her shoulders, he traced the curve of her lower lip with his tongue.

'Theo...'

'It's no good warning me not to tease you when I'm already addicted.' The hands that had settled just above her waist slipped lower, to cup her buttocks, and, lifting her gently, he rolled her against him so she could feel the power of his erection.

'You're so unfair...'

'Are you complaining?' Slipping the robe from her shoulders, he swung her into his arms and carried her to the bed. 'And, look, we're making progress.'

'Progress?'

'We made it to the bed...'

'Theo!'

'Miranda! I'm here. I'm not going anywhere...'

Theo was at her side in a moment, cradling her in his arms like a baby as she woke from the nightmare, and Miranda held him tightly, as if the closeness they had recaptured could all disappear as quickly as her dream. 'You didn't leave me?'

'Leave you?' He stared into her eyes. 'Of course not. You were having a nightmare, that's all. Can you remember what it was about?'

She couldn't believe it had happened again—not now, with Theo lying beside her. Worse still, she had woken from the dream still calling out.

'Did I say anything you could understand?' Acting unconcerned, she forced a bright note into her voice.

He answered carefully. 'Why do you ask?'

She sighed dismissively, staring directly at him, as if she

wanted to reassure him. 'I must have been dreaming about the accident again.'

'The details will fade in time.'

She couldn't hide the flicker of doubt, of pain, and this time Theo refused to let her slip away.

'No more secrets, Miranda,' he reminded her, still holding her gaze. 'What happened that you haven't told me about?'

She blenched, started to say something, then stalled. Her voice barely made it above a whisper, but he held back from pushing her, sensing that it would achieve nothing. To his relief she drew a deep ragged breath and tried again.

'He encouraged me to call him Papa.'

'Who did? Your teacher?'

'That's right.' She met his gaze again. 'And I did call him Papa, because I grew to think of him as a second father. I trusted him…completely.'

'And what happened to break that trust?'

As she grimaced it turned her face ugly, and her pain ran through him like a knife.

'That night…while we were driving…he reached for me.'

He went still. She surprised him with her calmness, and even more with the way she was still able to hold his gaze. But he felt that if he turned away now it would destroy her.

'We were driving down a busy road,' she continued, 'when suddenly he reached out his hand, laid it on my thigh, and then started to slip it higher, beneath my skirt. I was so shocked I lashed out… It was my fault the accident happened, Theo. A man was killed because of me.'

'No,' he said fiercely. Cupping her chin, he made her look at him. 'Your teacher was the only one at fault. The accident happened because of his greed and his inappropriate feelings towards you. He wanted too much of you, Miranda. He wanted all of you. He abused the trust placed in him by the college, by your family, and by you—'

'But if that's true then why do I feel so guilty? Maybe I led him on. I don't know—'

'But *I* know.' He fixed her with his stare, willing his certainty into her, knowing he had listened to her since the day they had met but he hadn't heard a word she was saying. He hadn't seen the injuries that cut far deeper than the damage to her arm. 'You did nothing wrong.' He spoke slowly and deliberately. 'You are the victim, Miranda, not the one at fault.' He held her gaze until she relaxed. But he made no move to touch her, to reassure her, because that belief had to come from inside her, not from him.

'It taught me something, Theo.'

'What?'

'Desire doesn't equal love.'

He smiled sadly, because she spoke so seriously about a truth that anyone who hadn't fallen beneath the shadow of a sexual predator would already know. 'I know that,' he said gently.

'So if the sex between us wasn't so good, you'd still love me?' She stared at him with concern.

'But it is good…' He wasn't sure how best to console her, or what to say, but he did know that what she'd confided in him was key to her happiness, her wellbeing, and to everything that made her whole as a person.

And if he had to pull back from the physical side of their life to give her time to heal, then he would.

'Did you mean it when you said you would take me to Athens to see another specialist?'

He thought his heart would explode with happiness. 'Of course.'

'What if it doesn't work?'

'Then we'll have tried.'

'You make it sound so straightforward.'

'Because it is straightforward. You have to try, unless you want to spend the rest of your life asking yourself *What if?*'

'All right,' she said hesitantly.

'Where is your violin now, by the way?'

'It's with Alessandro and Emily in Ferara. I asked them to keep it for me…until I was ready to play it again. It's in safe-keeping,' she added, brightening, 'and that's all that matters.'

That was *not* all that mattered, Theo reflected tensely. However valuable and precious the violin might be, it was still an object that could be replaced; Miranda, his wife, his heart, his love, could never be replaced.

When the yacht slipped into its berth on Kalmos, Theo dispatched his staff to help Agalia and Spiros with the preparations for the blessing.

Since she had told him the truth about the accident Miranda felt their relationship had shifted into another gear. Theo had changed towards her. He had become focused on the operation he believed would repair her arm, and had spent hours on the telephone to Athens. When he was with her he was gentle, and considerate—as he might be with a sickly relative—which was not what she wanted from him.

Was he repulsed by her complicity in her teacher's death? He had seemed so genuine when they'd talked about it—but maybe he'd had time to think things through since then? Maybe he had come to believe that she had played some part in the sexual game? It was all such a tangle in her mind. There was too much emotion involved. Too much had happened, and so quickly…

To add fuel to her concerns, Theo had backed away from her sexually. Maybe it was because of her secret, maybe he just felt sorry for her, but either way he was keeping her at a distance. He was treating her like a patient, not a person, acting as if she might break, or as if pity—either that or disgust—had replaced passion in his mind.

She couldn't rid herself of the feeling that she was unworthy to be his wife, that she had let him down, and, to add to her sense of isolation, within minutes of approaching harbour he said he had a business appointment arranged for when they docked. She knew then that she had to get away. She needed time to think, time alone…time to get used to being alone.

It was a simple matter to slip down the bustling gangplank unnoticed. She walked swiftly, head down, towards the town, crossing the paved esplanade that skirted the beach and walking on to where she could see the small apartment block, blindingly white in the midday sun.

Theo was right. She had floated with the current long enough. There was a public telephone booth just inside the swing doors where she would settle her mind and then make a call to Ferara.

When his meeting drew to a successful conclusion Theo was buoyed up with plans and eager to make a start. The jet was already fuelled and waiting for them on the tarmac. The appointment with the specialist had been made. Having talked to the surgeon who had obtained Miranda's medical records, he was hopeful.

He had to be hopeful; he was an optimist by nature. That was the character trait upon which he had built an empire. If the operation on her arm and hand went wrong, if the doctors really couldn't help her, then that same optimism would show him how to blunt her disappointment and help her through it.

The optimism vanished when he went back on board the yacht.

'What do you mean, my wife isn't here?' Theo felt the blood drain from his face.

'No one has seen Kyria Savakis since we docked.'

Theo stared at the member of crew unlucky enough to deliver this piece of news. 'Then search again!'

'Yes, sir.'

He had given instructions that Miranda's every wish should be accommodated, so what had gone wrong?

He marched into his office and stared at the envelope on the desk. His name was written on it in Miranda's unmistakable script. Ripping it open, he scanned the page.

> *I just need a bit of time. I have to find myself, Theo, and I need help. I can't ask you to do that for me...*

How could she still doubt him? Did she think he was incapable of love? He had thought that once...but now he had to go after her. Tightening his fist around the paper, he tossed it in the bin.

Calls to Ferara from a small island in the Greek archipelago were anything but straightforward, Miranda discovered. She had only just got her head round the complex dialling system when she spotted Theo coming towards her across the sand. Replacing the receiver, she stood back in the shadows. Her stomach clenched and unclenched. She felt as if she was balanced precariously on a knife's edge and her entire hope of happiness rested on that blade. He must have called at the taverna first, and now he was homing in on the only other place on the island to which logic had told him she would return.

Pushing through the doors, she stood waiting for him.

'*Theos*, Miranda! What are you doing here?'

'I wanted to speak to Emily—'

'Emily?' He stared at her, his expression a taut mix of anger and confusion. 'You leave me a note saying you have to find yourself, and that I can't do that for you, and then you come here to call your sister? Do you think Emily can succeed where I have so obviously failed?'

'Theo, please. It isn't like that.'

'Then what is it like, Miranda? Explain to me, please. Because I don't understand.'

'You've done so much for me already—'

'Don't talk to me as if I'm a casual acquaintance whose cup of kindness is running out. I'm your husband, Miranda, and I love you. Don't shut me out. Don't turn to your twin first. Emily has her own life to lead, and we have ours—'

'Do we? *Do we*, Theo? You've hardly spoken to me since I told you the truth about the accident. And you haven't touched me since!'

'I haven't touched you because I respect you too much—'

'That sounds like a cop-out, Theo—as if you couldn't bear to touch me once you knew the truth.'

'What do you want of me, Miranda? If I give you space, you think I'm ignoring you; if I try to help you, you push me away…'

As Theo raked his hair in a familiar gesture Miranda shook her head. 'I just thought if I spoke to Emily…' Her voice tailed away.

As he held her gaze she could see the truth reflected in his eyes, and her reasons seemed so thin suddenly, like a chimera brought on by insecurities left over from another life; a chimera as insubstantial as the morning mist that burned away so swiftly in the face of the sun.

'You couldn't call your sister from the yacht? Have you any idea how worried I've been?'

'I didn't want to disturb you. You were busy…'

'So you turned to your sister, when *I* am here for you?'

Miranda stared at him and realised he was right. Why had she blanked him out? Was she so afraid of risking her heart?

'Do you know how many people I've got looking for you? Couldn't you have told someone you meant to leave the yacht? Couldn't you have spoken to me first?'

Reaching up, she stopped him, caressing his face. For a few seconds neither of them spoke, and then, capturing her hand, Theo brought it to his lips.

'I know I've been preoccupied, but I never meant to ignore you,' he said. 'And it wasn't just the accident that made me draw back. When I'm on the trail of something I don't know how to let go. Truth is, I've been trying to organise a surprise for you.'

'A surprise?'

'I know I've been clumsy…will you forgive me?' His lips tugged up ruefully, but then he frowned. 'You may not like your surprise.'

'Try me.'

'It's not very romantic.'

'Theo! What is it?'

'A visit to a consultant in Athens. I warned you it wasn't very romantic.' He waited tensely to see what she would say.

Miranda shook her head, beginning to smile. 'You've got an original take on just about everything, Theo.'

'So I'm a romantic now?' His tongue was firmly planted in his cheek.

'You're something,' she said, turning her face up for his kiss.

CHAPTER FOURTEEN

THE prognosis was better than Miranda had dared to hope. The Athens surgeon felt confident she would regain most of the flexibility she had lost in her fingers, and that her arm would straighten if she underwent the appropriate physiotherapy once her elbow was reset. She would never play the violin professionally again, but she could teach—and that was all that mattered if her plans were to come to fruition.

She was sitting across from Theo in a capacious and very comfortable leather armchair on board his jet on their return journey to Kalmos, wishing she knew what he was thinking. The hospital visit had turned him serious again. He was all purpose and practicality, setting dates for the operation and for the follow-up treatment, and now he was making notes in his diary.

'You're not turning me into a business, are you?'

His gaze flicked up and he gave her a slow smile. 'Not turning…you *are* my business.'

As another judder set everything rattling Miranda braced her feet against the floor, as if by sheer force of will she could hold the giant aircraft in the air. What she needed was a distraction, and the attendants *had* been told not to disturb them. Peering out of the window, she decided they must be at least a mile high. 'Theo…?'

'Miranda? Is there something I can do for you?'

'Maybe…'

'Only maybe?' Theo cocked his head to slant a glance at her.

She decided to go for the direct approach, but the plane chose that moment to buck, and so she yelped instead, and pressed back in her seat.

'Why are you shaking?'

'You know I hate flying.'

'Then I shall have to see what I can do to change that. Chess?' Theo suggested, reaching into a pocket by the seat.

'No. Theo.'

He shrugged. 'Then do you have any other ideas?'

'Do *you* have any idea how annoying you can be?'

'I have some idea.' Standing up, he held out his hand to her. Miranda shrank into her seat. 'Is it safe to be walking around while there's turbulence like this?'

'No, you're right.' He frowned, and appeared to consider her suggestion. 'You'll be much safer lying down…'

The bed in Theo's jet was firm and wide, and the journey back from Athens taught Miranda more than most people ever got the chance to learn about turbulence. It removed her anxiety about the appointment, and gave her something else to concentrate on other than the physics of flight—which remained, as always, a mystery to her.

'Do you feel better now?' Theo held her close as the jet made its final descent.

'Are you ticking off my hang-ups one by one?' Miranda demanded, and then whimpered as his searching fingers found her again.

'I'm sorry—I have to punish you for finding me out.'

'Don't apologise,' she gasped.

'Look at me, Miranda,' he ordered. 'There isn't much time. We're coming in to land…just keep looking at me.'

'Are these doors soundproof?' Miranda asked, when she had calmed down enough to speak.

'Totally,' Theo promised.

'That's a relief.'

'And now we really do have to get out of bed—unless, of course, you'd like to stay here overnight?'

'Tempting as that is…'

'So what do you think about flying now?'

'I think I'm a convert.'

Theo made sure that Miranda's reunion with her family on the deck of his yacht was a very special occasion. She had never felt so alive, she realised, as she watched him talking easily to her sister's husband, Prince Alessandro.

'They have a lot in common,' Emily observed shrewdly, following her sister's gaze.

'Probably friends in common,' Miranda agreed. 'After all, they move in similar circles.'

'I was thinking more of their wives…'

'Us?' Miranda grinned into jade-green eyes that mirrored her own. 'Of course. Poor them.'

'It can't be easy for them. No wonder they feel the need to compare notes.'

'But you're happy, aren't you, Emily?'

'What do you think?' Emily traced the contours of her expanding waistline. 'I love my new country, my husband, and his adorable father. And with an heir and a spare, and now another baby on the way, I'm not the only one who's happy. There's Alessandro's father… Doesn't that smile speak volumes?'

They both smiled and waved at the distinguished older man who was presently talking to their mother.

'Family life is perfect. Alessandro is happy, I'm happy, his father's happy, and the dynasty is assured.'

'And you don't mind the dynastic element? The restrictions imposed by such a high-profile life?'

'Should I?'

'No, it's just that—'

'I'm a career woman? I have a thriving practice? I have never given up the law. It's a balancing act, Miranda; you'll get the hang of it.'

'Do you really think so?'

'I'm sure of it. What did we always say to each other? The most important thing is for a woman to retain her independence in here…' She tapped her head. 'That doesn't stop you loving someone, or having a family. And, with men like Alessandro and Theo, how could you resist doing either?'

'Only with the greatest difficulty,' Miranda agreed, beginning to laugh.

'You know, there was a time when I wondered if I would ever see you laugh again. He's good for you, Miranda.'

'You knew, didn't you? About my arm?'

'When I visited you in the hospital I could see the prognosis in your eyes before the doctors said a word to us.'

Miranda ground her jaw. 'I'm such a fool, Em. You all knew…the doctors told you. I should have known.'

'Yes…but you didn't want to talk about it, and we respected that. We wanted to give you space. Tell me we did the right thing?'

'Don't you start feeling guilty. I should have said something. I should have come straight to you—or Mum and Dad.'

'I'd say your behaviour was completely understandable. It was a terrible shock.'

'Maybe, but I shouldn't have run away to Greece—'

'But aren't you glad you did?' Emily slanted a mischievous smile at her twin as she gazed across at the two striking men, talking together at the bow rail. 'Just as I'm glad I had to take your place on stage the night I met Alessandro.'

The sisters barely had time to exchange a smile before their mother bore down on them.

'Darlings, we must move to the aft deck…'

Mrs Weston was in her element, complete with large-brimmed hat topped off with a flurry of violet feathers.

'Calm down, Mother,' Miranda said, smiling. 'It's not like this is the first wedding you've ever attended.'

'No, but it's my first blessing on board a billionaire's yacht.'

'Your mother's right in this instance, Miranda…'

'All right. I give in, Dad.' She wasn't going to escape, Miranda realised happily as her father took her arm.

There was quite a crowd gathering on the aft deck. She could see Agalia and Spiros being ushered forward to a place of honour alongside Lexis and Alessandro's father. 'What's going on?'

'This is my wedding present to you,' Theo said, stepping forward.

Miranda's face broke into a smile. 'What is it? What's happening?' she said excitedly, staring up at him as her parents relinquished their hold on her.

'Wait and see,' he said mysteriously, as a pathway cleared for them.

And then she saw the young Chinese girl standing on an improvised stage in front of all their wedding guests. Wearing a simple sky-blue dress, the slender girl was barely in her teens. 'I don't understand—'

Putting his finger over his lips, Theo led her towards the two chairs at the centre of the front row. 'You will in a minute. I promise,' he whispered with a smile.

As soon as they were settled, Alessandro, Prince of Ferara,

Emily's husband, stepped forward with some ceremony. He was carrying her violin. Bowing low, he presented it to her.

'Li Chin is waiting to play her audition piece for you, Miranda.'

'Oh, Theo…'

The beautiful old instrument seemed to come alive in Miranda's hands without a string being touched. It was a powerful symbol of how far they'd both come.

'This is for you,' he said quietly.

'This is for both of us,' she corrected him. 'How can I ever tell you what this means to me, or how much I love you?'

'You can make a start the moment Li Chin has finished her recital,' Theo promised dryly.

'Have we found our first exciting talent?' he asked, the moment Li Chin had finished playing.

'Yes. Li Chin has a remarkable talent. I don't remember hearing anyone quite like her before.'

'No?' Theo demanded softly. 'I do…'

Miranda smiled, and then stood with their guests to applaud the gifted girl.

'I think this scholarship programme's going to run and run,' Theo confided above the cheers.

'For ever?' Miranda demanded, holding his gaze.

'Oh, I should imagine a lot longer than that…'

REQUEST YOUR FREE BOOKS!

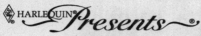

2 FREE NOVELS PLUS 2
FREE GIFTS!

YES! Please send me 2 FREE Harlequin Presents® novels and my 2 FREE gifts.
After receiving them, if I don't wish to receive any more books, I can return the shipping
statement marked "cancel." If I don't cancel, I will receive 6 brand-new novels every
month and be billed just $3.80 per book in the U.S., or $4.47 per book in Canada, plus
25¢ shipping and handling per book and applicable taxes, if any*. That's a savings of
close to 15% off the cover price! I understand that accepting the 2 free books and gifts
places me under no obligation to buy anything. I can always return a shipment and
cancel at any time. Even if I never buy another book from Harlequin, the two free books
and gifts are mine to keep forever.

106 HDN EEXK   306 HDN EEXV

Name _____ (PLEASE PRINT) _____

Address _____ Apt. # _____

City _____ State/Prov. _____ Zip/Postal Code _____

Signature (if under 18, a parent or guardian must sign)

Mail to the **Harlequin Reader Service®**:
IN U.S.A.: P.O. Box 1867, Buffalo, NY 14240-1867
IN CANADA: P.O. Box 609, Fort Erie, Ontario L2A 5X3

Not valid to current Harlequin Presents subscribers.

Want to try two free books from another line?
Call 1-800-873-8635 or visit www.morefreebooks.com.

* Terms and prices subject to change without notice. NY residents add applicable sales tax.
Canadian residents will be charged applicable provincial taxes and GST. This offer is limited to
one order per household. All orders subject to approval. Credit or debit balances in a customer's
account(s) may be offset by any other outstanding balance owed by or to the customer. Please allow
4 to 6 weeks for delivery.

Your Privacy: Harlequin is committed to protecting your privacy. Our Privacy
Policy is available online at www.eHarlequin.com or upon request from the Reader
Service. From time to time we make our lists of customers available to reputable
firms who may have a product or service of interest to you. If you would
prefer we not share your name and address, please check here. ☐

**From the magnificent Blue Palace to the wild
plains of the desert, be swept away as three
sheikh princes find their brides.**

Proud and passionate...
Three billionaires are soon to discover
the truth to their ancestry...

Wild and untamed...
They are all heirs to the throne of
the desert kingdom of Kharastan...

*Though royalty is their destiny, these sheikhs
are as untamed as their homeland!*

Don't miss any of the books
in this brand-new trilogy from

Sharon Kendrick!

THE SHEIKH'S ENGLISH BRIDE,
Book #2612, Available March 2007
THE SHEIKH'S UNWILLING WIFE,
Book #2620, Available April 2007
THE DESERT KING'S VIRGIN BRIDE,
Book #2628, Available May 2007

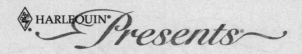

HARLEQUIN *Presents*

Coming Next Month

#2611 ROYALLY BEDDED, REGALLY WEDDED Julia James
By Royal Command
Lizzy Mitchell is an ordinary girl, but she has something Prince Rico Renaldi wants: the heir to the throne of his principality! Lizzy is the heir's adoptive mother, and she will do anything to keep her son. Then Rico demands a marriage of convenience....

#2612 THE SHEIKH'S ENGLISH BRIDE Sharon Kendrick
The Desert Princes
When billionaire Xavier de Maistre discovers he could inherit the kingdom of Kharastan, it's a surprise. But more surprising is Laura Cottingham, the lawyer who delivered the news. Xavier wants her, but is she ready to be tamed and tempted by this desert prince?

#2613 THE ITALIAN BOSS'S SECRETARY MISTRESS Cathy Williams
Mistress to a Millionaire
Rose is in love with her gorgeous boss, Gabriel Gessi, but her resolve to forget him crumbles when he demands they work closely together...on a Caribbean island! She knows the sexy Italian is the master of persuasion, and it won't be long before he's added her to his agenda.

#2614 THE KOUVARIS MARRIAGE Diana Hamilton
Wedlocked!
Madeleine is devastated to learn that her gorgeous Greek billionaire husband, Dimitri Kouvaris, only married her to conceive a child! She begs for divorce, but Dimitri is determined to keep Maddie at his side—and in his bed—until she bears the Kouvaris heir.

#2615 THE PRINCE'S CONVENIENT BRIDE Robyn Donald
The Royal House of Illyria
Prince Marco Considine knows he's met his match when he meets model Jacoba Sinclair. But Jacoba has a secret: she is Illyrian, just like Prince Marco, a fact that could endanger her life. Marco seizes a perfect opportunity to protect her—by announcing their engagement!

#2616 WANTED: MISTRESS AND MOTHER Carol Marinelli
Ruthless!
Ruthless barrister Dante Costello hires Matilda Hamilton to help his troubled little girl. An intense attraction flares between them, and Dante decides he will offer Matilda the position of mistress. But what Dante thought was lust turns out to be something far greater.

#2617 THE SPANIARD'S MARRIAGE DEMAND Maggie Cox
A Mediterranean Marriage
Leandro Reyes could have any girl he wanted. Only in the cold light of morning did Isabella realize she was just another notch on his belt. But their passionate night together was to have a lasting consequence Leandro couldn't ignore. His solution: to demand that Isabella marry him!

#2618 THE CARLOTTA DIAMOND Lee Wilkinson
Dinner at 8
Charlotte Christie had no idea that the priceless diamond necklace she wore on her wedding day meant more than she realized. But Simon Farringdon didn't see her innocence until too late. What would happen when Charlotte discovered the Carlotta Diamond was his only motive for marriage?

HPCNM0207